Dirty Hoe

A GARDENING ROMANCE

SMALL TOWN DIRT
BOOK ONE

REGINA BERGEN

In loving memory of my mom, the strongest and kindest woman I've ever met—and the woman who taught me never to judge another until you've walked a mile in their shoes.

And for my dad, who has lifted me up and supported me through some of the toughest challenges of my life, especially over the past several years. I don't know where I'd be without him.

Special thanks to Kate Seger, my sister and fellow author, who cheered me on and guided me through every step of the writing, editing, and publishing process. Without Kate, this book simply wouldn't exist—and I never would have embarked on my own writing adventure.

Goodbye, Boys!

GIA

Chapter 1

"You know what? If we could all just sew our damn red flags together and wear them like capes, it'd make this whole bullshit online dating thing infinitely easier—for all of us!" Gia shoved her gloved fingers into the dirt, the plastic claws on the end easily splitting through the small roots in her way. She wasn't talking to anyone in particular; no one else was there, after all. But she continued her rant all the same.

"Put it *all* out there for *everyone* to see—to take it or leave it. At least we would know what we're getting involved in before it's too late!" She scoffed, haphazardly pulling weeds out and chucking them over her shoulder into a rapidly growing pile.

She'd worry about them later. "Married!" she muttered. "He was *married*." She emphasized the last word with an angry huff.

Newly divorced, but after a long, frustrating process, Gia finally felt ready to dip her toes into the dating world, and thus far, it hadn't been the experience she'd hoped for. The dating pool felt more like a cesspool, and she was about to give up on the whole damn thing. Her first date repertoire now included, but wasn't limited to, married men whose wives had no idea they were perusing dating sites, ethical polygamists, seekers of friends with benefits, fuckboys, stalkers, and a host of other types she wasn't looking for.

"Whatever floats your boat, really—but mine is sinking!" she mumbled under her breath. "I should just stay single. Date myself. At least I know I'm faithful and honest. The body could use a little work, though," she chuckled. At least she could still laugh at herself and the situation. *Mom bod*, she thought. *If 'dad bod' was a thing, why couldn't 'mom bod' be?*

She knew at least some men found her attractive despite the extra weight she still carried around after three kids and years of personal neglect. Thick thighs and pretty eyes. That's how one man had described it; it was accurate if she was honest. Finding men who thought she was at least decent-looking wasn't the issue. She just couldn't seem to find men with the qualities *she* desired who also wanted some level of exclusivity and commitment.

At first, it wasn't a problem. Newly single, Gia had merely wanted to play for a while and to discover what she wanted, didn't want, liked, didn't like, and so on. *She* was the one who didn't want more. She wasn't looking for exclusivity or longevity then, but somewhere along the line, it all got old. Hookups, one-night stands, friends with benefits, and situationships began to feel empty and lacking. Sure, she felt empowered and sexy, but then there was nothing to hold onto. No support, no comfort, no relationship.

It wasn't enough. Gia had learned that lesson the hard way

after falling for one of the "FWB" guys she had been seeing regularly. The sex was incredible, but Gia wanted more than that after a few months. He didn't. It hurt. It was not a catastrophic, soul-crushing pain, but it certainly wasn't pleasant, and she had no intention of doing it again.

She scooped up a fistful of dirt and allowed it to fall through her fingers, covering several tiny seeds she had pressed gently into the ground below. Gardening was her peace. Her tranquility. The garden itself, her sanctuary. She had designed it to provide a sense of calm and harmony with nature—a space to escape the outside world and disappear into her own thoughts amidst the flowers, herbs, vegetables, bees, butterflies, and beautiful surroundings. She needed that peace now more than ever!

If she was going to date now, it would be men who wanted more than to get laid. Maybe it would take a while to find the right one, but she wouldn't waste her time on the ones she *knew* were wrong from the jump anymore.

Gia abruptly rose from her knees and stood, arms folded across her chest. "That's it! I'm re-evaluating my priorities. I don't need any man!" She gazed at the garden before her, the breathtaking result of her hard work and commitment. She had her kids, dogs, garden, and home. And she had kept it all together —alive and thriving—for an entire year on her own, quite possibly the most challenging year of her life. *I'm fine on my own. So, why am I rushing this?*

With that, Gia pulled out her cell phone and tapped open the folder appropriately titled "Dating B.S." Then, one by one, she deleted the dating apps she'd spent countless hours browsing profiles and swiping left or right on.

"Goodbye, boys! I've had enough. I'm on my own now!" As the determined words sprung from her lips, she hit the tiny 'x' hovering just over the last remaining dating apps.

It was official: Gia was stepping out of the dating world!

Dating P.S

GIA

Chapter 2

GIA FELT overwhelming fear and relief as she erased the last app from her phone. She would no longer have it as a fallback when feeling low. Men who wanted to get in her pants would say anything to do it, and she'd let herself believe them when she needed a boost. It had been her crutch for over a year when she wasn't feeling confident or empowered. Chat with some random guy, let him build her up, then find something wrong with him and bail.

She supposed the correct term was "ghosting," but she preferred to reserve that phrase for pulling a disappearing act on someone she had already physically met—like, in person. Online guys were just prospects, and most would never become anything more. Initially, she'd never even considered just fading out mid-conversation with someone when it wasn't perfect, but it had been done to her so many times that it became no big deal somewhere along the way.

Just another reason the dating apps had to go. They were making her less considerate of others, hiding behind her phone and not forcing her to have difficult conversations aloud. No repercussions!

Gia kneeled back down and returned to weeding, carefully pulling only those plants that didn't belong. She almost felt guilty yanking out the poor, fast-growing plants whose only mistake had been to grow in her herb bed rather than a few feet to one side or the other. To her, there was nothing wrong with a weed in and of itself—only when it got in the way of her lavender, sage, oregano, or whatever other plant it was stealing nutrients from in any given space.

In a way, they were like the men who had dared enter her life —for however briefly—over the past year. Some were okay, likable even, and maybe under different circumstances, she would have let them stay... but it was merely a long trail of wrong times, places, and men. And she was done.

As her mind wandered, her eyes suddenly flew open wide. "Dammit!" she shouted, raising a fist wrapped around a thin-leafed plant capped with purple flowers. "That was *not* a weed," she muttered, eyes narrowing as she eyed the sprig of lavender she held, roots and all.

She had been babying that particular plant from a tiny seed and was waiting for it to take root and spread. Instead, she'd just plucked it from the ground. "Shit!" she exclaimed.

"Whatcha swearing about?" a female voice rang out cheerily from the other side of a tall, white fence separating her yard from the next-door neighbor's.

"Carla, turn that chipperness down a notch, or we're gonna have a problem," Gia said dully, side-eyeing the lavender in her hand, then shifting her eyes to the fence. She placed the plant down gently on the side of the raised bed, committing to replanting it and attempting to save it later on.

"Oh, excellent. I see your garden of tranquility is having a very calming effect on you this morning." Sarcasm oozed out with every word.

Carla pushed a loose fence post to the side and squeezed through into Gia's backyard.

"Perhaps not inviting calm today as much as... inciting clarity!" Gia responded, touching her chin thoughtfully. "In the aftermath of last night's shit storm of a date, I've made a decision."

Carla perched herself on the edge of one of Gia's raised garden beds and tilted her head, listening intently. "What happened last night? And what'd you decide?" Carla rested her elbows on her knees and her head in her hand.

"Remember Marco? The guy I was talking to online?"

"Yeah. The one with the dark hair and blue eyes. I remember him. I remember him well." Carla winked. "Go on." She nodded slowly, rolling her hand in a circular 'continue' gesture, clearly waiting in anticipation for the always-juicy details of yet another dating story.

Gia had to chuckle. Carla had been her next-door neighbor since Gia and her ex-husband, Steven, had moved in over a decade ago. He was long gone, but their friendship continued—and she knew it always would. Carla tapped her wrist, indicating the time was ticking away, and the story remained untold. In some ways, Gia thought Carla enjoyed her online dating exploits significantly more than she herself did.

"Okay, okay. I'm getting there," Gia responded. "Marco, as it turns out, is married!"

"Like, in an open marriage?"

"Nope. No, no, no. A plain, old, stereotypical, monogamous marriage, in theory, anyway. Obviously, not in practice. The type of marriage in which the wife doesn't have even the faintest clue that her husband is browsing dating sites while she's doing the dishes. The kind where she calls in the middle of the date and goes completely off the rails—fairly so—because her friend sees him from across the bar sitting with another woman—me. *That* type of married."

"Ooooh, shit. *That* type of married. I'm sorry, girl."

"For fuck's sake, Carla. What does a woman have to do to find a decent man who wants a relationship and who isn't a cheating bastard?" Carla merely shrugged. "Which brings me to my next point," Gia continued. "I'm done! Officially, one hundred percent done and out of this dating game nonsense."

"Are you, though?" Carla asked, knowing she'd heard this all before.

"I am! This one takes the cake. He was *married*! Apps are deleted. Profiles erased. I'm dating myself from here on out! I'm closed for business."

As Gia spoke, she raised her phone to eye-level with Carla, swiping the screen on to illustrate the intentional disappearance of the 'Dating B.S.' folder. "See? Gone!"

An Abrupt Departure

GIA

Chapter 3

"WELL, this isn't one of your best dating stories, I must admit. I mean, it's a little anti-climactic if you think about it. Sure, he's married, but I'm willing to bet that 75% of the men on those sites are married or in "committed" relationships. I've already told you that. You didn't believe me until you saw it firsthand," Carla pointed out.

"You do realize I don't date solely for your entertainment, right? I'm not exactly going for the cinematic collapse of my romantic life." Gia rolled her eyes. "I'd actually like to find someone again someday. Somebody to settle down with and enjoy each other's company. We all know my marriage was a disaster from day one, before that even. I just want a chance to try again. For the time being, though, I'm done. I can't do it anymore." Gia let out an exasperated sigh. "I can't do the lies, the games, the bullshit. I just want someone I can find peace with... someone I like, my kids like, my dogs like. Am I asking for too much?"

"Nah. Perhaps too much from a dating site, though—at least the ones *you're* on!" Suddenly, Carla's eyes lit up momentarily, and Gia could tell she was trying to suppress some newly erupting excitement.

"Carla, what? No. I don't know what you're thinking of doing, but I can tell you right now, you better not do it. I know that look, and I don't want it. I don't want any of what it inevitably leads to. It never ends well. No!"

For as long as Gia had lived there, Carla had been scheming! Her mind was always in motion, from get-rich-quick plans and inventions to manipulating friends and relatives to get what she wanted from them. None of it was done out of malice, but things often didn't work out precisely as she planned—and sometimes, it was downright catastrophic.

She had an unnerving flashback to the time Carla had arranged a blind date with a "college guy" for her in high school, and it turned out to be a man attending circus school. He showed up in a full clown costume! He turned out to be a nice guy, but not exactly what she had hoped to get out of the date—and it gave awkward a whole new meaning. " Gia's thoughts continued to drift as she recalled the time Carla had decided they should start a "Babysitters Club" but didn't tell any of the participating children's parents. She simply took the kids from their yards, consolidating them at Gia's childhood home for arts and crafts. It caused an uproar—not to mention police involvement!

Gia *did not* want to be involved. Not again.

"I swear, I won't do anything to harm your life, Gia baby! You know I only want what's best for you." Carla smirked.

While Gia didn't love how Carla phrased that vow, she had no choice but to accept it and hope for the best—or pray she'd simply forget whatever hair-brained scheme had entered her mind when something more exciting came along.

"Can we change the subject now?" Gia asked with a sigh. "I don't want to talk about dating, men, or the opposite sex... Can we talk about gardening or something? Hey, toss me that hoe, will you?"

Carla grabbed the tool resting against the wooden garden bed she was still using as a seat and flipped it across the narrow path between beds, aiming the handle toward Gia. "Here you go. But, I, uh... I have to go now. Can't garden today, chicky! Have fun, though. I hope you find more clarity, or whatever."

Gia thought it strange that Carla would come through the fence and stay for such a short time. They often spent hours over the weekends watching the birds, bees, and butterflies after Gia finished her yard work. Sometimes Carla helped, others she didn't, but she was typically at least present and sharing a bottle of wine with her friend on the days Gia's children were with her ex-husband or playing with them on days they were there, too.

"Um, okay. See ya later, then." Gia stared after her friend in confusion as Carla hopped off the raised bed and moved back toward the fence line.

"Bye! I'll give you a call later."

Carla squeezed through the fence and replaced it behind her. They'd been visiting each other's yards this way for over ten years, and at this point, it would be odd for either of them to enter via ordinary means, like a gate or the front door! However, as Carla made it to the other side, Gia was almost certain she heard her gait shift from a walk to a run, moving toward her own home.

"This probably isn't good," Gia said aloud, raising her eyes and arms to the sky, beseeching the gods for mercy and begging them to keep Carla's interference in her love life to a minimum.

"Please. Please, please, please, let her mind her own business for once!"

Profile Pictures

CARLA

Chapter 4

CARLA DUCKED her head as she came through the fence, leaving Gia's yard. Once on the other side, out of Gia's line of vision, she took off toward her own house in a sprint. She knew Gia would *not* be on board with her brilliant idea, but she didn't care—it was in her best interest.

As she reached the back stairway leading up to her sliding glass door, she took the steps two by two, arriving on the small deck out of breath. *Oof, I need to get in shape.*

"Where's the fire?" Matt, her husband, asked as she sped past him. He was standing in front of the barbeque, grilling up some sort of meat that smelled absolutely delicious.

"No fire. Although, possibly not the best phrasing under the circumstances." She glanced at the flames nipping at the grates on the grill. "Just have to handle something on Gia's behalf," she added. Matt eyed her suspiciously, taking note of her tone of voice and expression and rolling his eyes.

"You know what... I don't even want to know. It's better if I don't. Try not to get yourself—or her— in too much trouble, though. She's had a rough year, you know?"

"Oh, I know. That's exactly why I'm doing this."

"What, exactly, is *this*, anyway? No, wait, never mind. Don't tell me. I said I wouldn't ask. I don't want to know," Matt said with renewed determination, turning back toward his grill.

"What're you making anyway? Meat?"

"I'll show you my meat." Matt winked flirtatiously at Carla and gently elbowed her in the ribs.

"No time for that now—but save me some of whatever that is. It smells incredible!"

"I see how it is. You only want me for my meat." Matt let out a faux exasperated sigh. As Carla spun away from him to head through the deck door, he gave her a good, solid slap on the behind.

"Love you," he called after her.

"Love you, too. See? This is why I'm doing this for Gia! She needs someone like you, a source of good old-fashioned ass slaps and meat," Carla said as Matt pretended to put his fingers in his ears and began humming.

"Don't—want—to—know!"

Carla rolled her eyes before dashing inside.

She stopped in the kitchen and poured herself a glass of wine before walking over to the couch, setting her laptop on the coffee table in front of her, opening it, and hitting the power button. As the computer booted up, she took a long sip of wine.

"Gia, I'm doing this for you..." She chuckled as she opened her social media account, then clicked and typed until she wound up on Gia's profile. From there, she went into the 'Pictures' folder and began browsing. She knew they were there somewhere... the gardening pictures. Where were the gardening pictures?

Boom! She scrolled down and saw a series of professional-quality photographs of Gia and her children in her garden. The session had been a gift from Carla to Gia the year before, right after Carla's ex-husband had left. It was supposed to represent the next chapter in the house—just the kids and Gia—and the photos came out fabulously.

Having expected the photo shoot to include only the children, Gia hadn't been prepared for any personal involvement beyond wrangling them and ensuring they behaved. She certainly hadn't dressed as she would have been had she known. Instead, she wore simple jeans that were tight enough to highlight her... assets... without looking desperate and a light blue button-down tank top that accentuated her strong arms and dipped just low enough in front to cause a man to look twice.

When Carla pulled the photographer aside and told her to get the children's mother into some shots, Gia looked like she would pass out! She clearly wasn't used to having her picture taken, and Carla knew she hadn't expected it. If she had, she probably would have turned down the whole thing! Regardless, Carla wanted Gia to be in those photos with her kids, and if scheming was the only way to make it happen, so be it. Scheming was kind of her 'thing,' anyway. Honestly, it should have been expected, but Gia wasn't on her A-game back then. She had a lot going on.

Throughout their entire lives, Gia had always been the one behind the camera—never in front. Even after Carla's interference, most of the photographs still included Gia and the kids, but that could be remedied easily enough! After all, anyone could use Photoshop these days, and Carla was pretty well-versed if she did say so herself.

Carla carefully browsed the photos, saving the five of them she thought made Gia look the best—and that would be easy to edit as needed—to her desktop. One by one, she opened the photos and got to work, removing the children from the images so they included only Gia and her breathtaking garden.

She looked each one over when she finished, admiring her handiwork.

"Not bad, Carla. Not bad at all," she said aloud, clearly impressed with herself. The words were just escaping her lips when Matt entered the room and approached her with a tray of food that sent an irresistible aroma wafting toward her. She opened her mouth to talk, but Matt placed his hand on her lips, effectively cutting her off.

"Shhh. I don't want to know. Let's eat," he said, pulling her up from the couch with his free hand and leading her into the kitchen.

"Will there be dessert?" she asked, winking at her husband.

"More meat," he said gruffly, kissing her on her neck, just behind her ear.

"My favorite," Carla responded, moving toward the kitchen with Matt. "Let's eat quickly so we can get to dessert."

Only Gardeners

CARLA

Chapter 5

CARLA LAY next to Matt in their king-sized bed. They were still breathing heavily from their post-lunch romp between the sheets. Carla couldn't help but feel thankful that her spouse was nothing like Gia's former husband. Matt was everything to her—a best friend, an incredible lover, and he even helped cook and clean up around the house. She wasn't sure how she got so lucky, but she knew Gia deserved the same things.

She needed someone with shared hobbies and interests—someone who liked gardening! And that was precisely what triggered her plan. There *had* to be a way for Gia to meet like-minded men who gardened or farmed or... something... without her knowing she was being set up. Gia needed to meet someone when she wasn't expecting it and have it unfold naturally, at least as far as she knew anyway.

Carla rolled over toward Matt, whose eyes had closed several minutes ago. A slight snore emerged as he exhaled, but that never bothered her. Some of her friends slept in different rooms from their spouses solely based on snoring, but she actually found the sound calming. It wasn't obnoxious at all. It reminded her of his presence at night, and she always knew she had someone there with her to get through the ups and downs life threw at her—someone who loved her just as much as she loved him. She rested her hand on his bare chest for a moment, feeling it rise and fall, then pressed her mouth against his cheek, giving him a short, sweet kiss.

Carla kicked her legs around to the side of the bed and rose to her feet, heading back to her computer to finish the task she had started earlier. She'd let him sleep. He deserved it after that lunch and that... dessert.

Several internet searches later, Carla found herself on Only-Gardeners.com, a dating site that catered to gardeners at all levels, from beginner to advanced. It didn't seem to be a particularly well-known or heavily used site compared to the more general online dating sites, but she'd worry about that later. Maybe she'd—they'd—get lucky. She was hoping to find at least a few local male gardeners!

Carla began creating Gia's profile, taking the garden photos she'd edited the kids out of and using them as Gia's profile pictures. Despite Gia's lack of preparation for those pictures, Carla had to admit she looked stunning! She was at her best whenever she was in the garden, whether tending plants, harvesting food, or even pulling weeds. Now, it was time to find a guy who felt the same—and would worship Gia for it!

"Ta-dah!" Carla exclaimed. "Perfecto." The profile was complete, featuring several photos and all of Gia's interests and passions laid out. The only caveat was that Gia wouldn't be communicating with the men who were interested in her, not yet anyway. For once, she'd only be allowed to meet the fully vetted men who were absolutely bursting with green flags. Carla would make sure of it.

She hadn't exactly figured out all of the details, like, for example, what she'd do when she *did* find the right guy. She had no idea how she'd arrange the meet-up or if she would tell Gia or... or what. That seemed like a later problem. For now, she could only focus on one thing at a time.

Just as she hit "complete" on the profile, Matt walked in and glanced at the screen. Seeing the open dating profile with Gia's image front and center, he clucked his tongue at Carla.

"You didn't... Please tell me you didn't," Matt implored his wife.

"Well, I did. But I can explain! This is going to work, Matt. It's a site for gardeners! She hasn't tried this yet." Carla's attempts to convince Matt seemed to be falling on deaf ears. He had already started walking toward the kitchen to do the dishes they'd ditched in the sink earlier in the name of "dessert."

"Matt! It's going to work. Mark my words!"

"Sure, sure." Matt turned the water on as high as it would go.

"It—"

"What? I'm sorry. I can't seem to hear you. The running water must be too loud. I simply *must* finish these dishes so my lovely wife doesn't have to do them," Matt said.

Carla sighed in response but left him alone. She wasn't about to buy herself a sink full of dishes because she couldn't keep her mouth shut.

Carla knew he sometimes got frustrated with her crazy plans and scheming, but this one really *was* going to work—and her heart was in the right place. Gia needed something special in her life. She needed her very own Matt, and come hell of high water, Carla would find him for her!

Just then, Carla's cell phone buzzed. She picked it up and glanced at the front of the screen.

"Crap, it's Gia," she muttered, tossing her phone down onto

the couch like it was a creepy bug that had startled her in one swift motion.

"And? Will you be answering the phone, my little schemestress?" Matt chuckled. "Heh, shemestress. I like that. It's like... seamstress, but not." Carla loved it when Matt told a joke or one-liner but felt the need to explain it to be sure others got it. She thought it was adorable.

"Oh, sure, *now* you can hear everything." Carla tried to hide her smile. "I can't," she added.

"And why is that?"

"Because... she'll ask me what I'm doing."

"And?"

"And I can't lie to her—but I also can't tell her the truth right now."

"So, you're going to ignore her? For how long?"

Carla rubbed her chin thoughtfully. "I'm not sure. Maybe just until I get things all set up on this," she said, gesturing to the open screen before her. "Until I'm doing something else— anything else."

"Oh, Carla, Carla, Carla," Matt repeated. "Will you ever learn, my love?"

Carla let out a laugh. They both knew the answer was a resounding no.

Blast from the Past

CARLA

CARLA GLANCED AT MATT, who was doing his best to ignore his wife's shenanigans. He was passing a vacuum back and forth over the same area of floor over and over, listening to the dinging sound of dating app notifications from Carla's laptop. Carla tried to conceal her smile as he asked questions, indicating his interest in the situation. "Who was that?" he asked.

"A guy named... ew. Boris. That is *not* a gardener's name."

"Uh, I don't think gardeners get to hand-choose their names. It's not his fault his parents named him Boris. What does he look like? And what would a *gardener's* name be?"

Carla stared thoughtfully at her screen for a moment. "Hmm... maybe... Gus?"

"Gus? Whatever. What does Boris look like?"

"He's not Gia's type."

"What's Gia's type, then?"

"Not Boris." Carla glanced at Matt, who had stopped pretending to vacuum and was standing behind the couch, staring at the computer screen. "Listen, either you're in or you're out. If you're in, sit your butt down and help me. If you're out—pretend to do chores somewhere else!"

Matt scoffed, but plopped himself down on the couch next to his wife. They both stared at the laptop screen. No more than ten minutes had passed since Carla had finished her friend's dating profile, and the messages and 'likes' were already flowing in.

"I don't know how I let you rope me into this," Matt said, raising his eyes to the ceiling. "I swore I didn't want to get involved—didn't want to know a thing about this!"

"And yet here you are." Carla smirked. "You know you want to help Gia just as much as I do. Like it or not, it'd make things easier if we could all hang out together with no one feeling like a third wheel."

"I do *not* feel like a third wheel. And if I did, I wouldn't hang out with you two. And, if you feel like I'm a third wheel, then maybe I won't from now on," Matt said, turning his head away to keep Carla from seeing the subtle hurt in his eyes.

"Awww, Matty, don't be butt hurt! I didn't mean it like that. I just meant it'd make things so much *easier*—like double dates and stuff." Carla reached behind her with both arms to wrap them around Matt's neck and pull him in closer to her. "I love you."

"I love you, too," he scoffed, still pretending to be offended but unable to hide the interest he had developed in the little project. "Okay, so, who do we have? Who are our options?" he asked, looking intently at the screen.

"Well," Carla started, "there's weird, creepy faux-hawk guy." She wrinkled her nose as she flipped through the photographs on the screen. "He does *not* look like the gardening type." She shrugged.

"No. No, he does not. Swipe left," Matt told her, and she nodded in response, swiping her finger left across the touchscreen on the computer.

"What about Mr. Too-Tight-Leather-Pants?" She chuckled, rolling her eyes. "These aren't the type of men I was expecting to find on here."

They continued to flip through the pictures, swiping left repeatedly, muttering "no" in unison. Several minutes later, they gave up.

"I need a break. This is exhausting. I see why Gia chose to take a step back from this nonsense," Carla said, moving the laptop aside and standing up. She glanced at her phone, which she had silenced, and considered calling Gia back.

As if he could read her mind, Matt interrupted her thoughts. "What're you going to tell her you've been doing all this time?" he asked, raising his eyebrows in question.

"I... I'm not sure. I'll rely on my expert question evasion skills or just change the subject. It's not like she needs to know what I'm doing twenty-four-seven."

"No—but you usually tell her anyway." Matt laughed.

"Ugh. I'll just tell her you and I were *busy*. She won't ask any more questions. She is so against men right now that she won't even want to know anything else," Carla said. It seemed like as good an excuse as any, and it wasn't a lie.

"Fair enough," Matt agreed. "Okay, let's take a break and reconvene in an hour."

Carla laughed out loud. "I think you may officially be even more into this than I am," she accused, the corners of her mouth rising into a grin.

"I don't know if you've noticed, but beyond you, I really don't have much of a life," he admitted, wrapping his arms around her waist and pulling her close.

"Oh, I've noticed, and I'm just fine with it. We have a beautiful life. Now, we need to make the same happen for Gia." Just as Carla finished her sentence, a loud ding signified a new notification from *Only Gardeners*, causing both to glance down at the still-opened computer.

Simultaneously, both of their jaws dropped. "Benjamin Marshall!?" Carla squealed, her eyebrows raising practically off her forehead.

"I thought he moved to another country to hug trees and save the planet or something?" Matt asked.

"He did. I guess he's back. And, man, did he 'glow up' during his travels!"

"You mean 'grow up?'"

"No. I meant what I said. The nerdy boy got hot!" Realizing immediately what she'd just said in the presence of her husband, she backtracked. "Not as hot as you. I mean for Gia. You know what I mean. I mean... I love you," she rambled, tripping over her words.

"Ordinarily, I might be offended. But, in this case, I very heterosexually agree that that man *is*, in fact, hot—for Gia, of course," Matt admitted. "What was the notification? Did he like us? I mean her. I mean, I don't know what I mean."

"He *messaged* us. Her." Carla froze as she read the message that appeared on the screen:

Hey Gia,

I know it's been a long time. I was surprised to see you on here. I had heard you'd gotten married. I'm glad you're still garden-ing. Can we meet to talk about what happened before I left for Brazil?

Ben

Carla and Matt looked perplexed.

"What happened before Brazil?" Carla asked aloud. "I didn't even know they talked when he lived here... and I thought I knew *everything* about Gia. This is *not* acceptable!"

"Carla, I can see where this is going. As usual, I will be the voice of reason and tell you right now—don't do it. Don't get involved. Don't meddle. This isn't just some random guy from the internet. There's obviously at least some type of history here, and it's not your place to put the puzzle together. If she didn't tell you, it was probably for a reason."

Carla waved Matt off. "Just a few messages to see where it goes. It's for Gia," she said and began typing a response.

Dear Ben,

It's lovely to hear from you. You look great. I am recently divorced. Which part of what happened before you left did you want to discuss?

Gia

"Carla, I'm telling you right now. This is a bad idea. You're going to dig a hole much deeper than any you've dug before, and you're risking a very good friendship," Matt advised.

"Matt, it's fine. It'll be fine. I'm just doing a little bit of research for the project. You were super into it until just a couple of minutes ago. This could be a critical positive development!"

"Or a terrible one. And can we please stop referring to it as 'the project'?"

"Sure, sure," she said, waving him off dismissively again. "Now, you're either in the Gia Project or out. If you're in, sit down and wait for his response. If you're out, will you please go make me a sandwich?" Her lips formed into a fake pout, but a smirk tugged at the corners of her mouth.

She knew he was in. Part of her was disappointed, though. She was hungry again and could have used a sandwich.

Another notification sound caused them to whip their heads around to face the screen. Matt let himself fall butt-first onto the couch. "I know I'm going to regret this," he muttered.

Secrets and Sandwiches

GIA

WHAT IS SHE DOING?

Carla never ignored her phone calls, and when she missed them for some reason, she always called back right away. It had been hours and nothing. She was almost tempted to pop over there and ensure everything was okay, but she didn't want to interrupt if she and Matt were... enjoying each other's company.

Truth be told, she felt a little awkward going over there lately without warning. It had never been like that before her divorce, but she sometimes felt like a third wheel now, so she often waited until Carla appeared in her yard or called rather than simply stopping by like she used to. She was a little sad about it but filed it under the heading "It is what it is" and made some simple life adjustments—no big deal.

Gia pulled out her phone and glanced at it. Alright, no more dating apps to waste precious time on—what else was she supposed to do? She had relied on that swiping motion for so long that she sometimes found she wasn't quite sure what to do with herself now. Her morning garden work was done. Carla was M.I.A. The kids were with their dad. And she'd already accomplished all she could think to do—and had enough motivation to start—inside the house. As a freelance blog writer and social media manager, among other odd writing and editing jobs here and there, there was always "something" to do, but she just couldn't focus on her work.

Gia sighed. "Now what?" she said aloud, glancing around her home. She headed into the kitchen to make a sandwich. She couldn't take the silence for another second, so she made three sandwiches, tossed them in plastic baggies, and walked out the front door toward Carla's house.

She considered taking the route through the fence, but given that Carla hadn't answered—or returned— her phone calls, Gia felt weird just appearing in the backyard. *Ew,* she thought. She didn't like how the dynamic had changed, even though, as far as she knew, she was the only one who even noticed it. She walked up the front steps and rang the doorbell.

It took a few moments, but finally, Carla appeared at the door. "Oh! Gia, hi, hello!" she greeted, seeming frazzled. "How's it going?"

"Uh. Okay. You're being weird. I called."

"Yeah, sorry! I was, uh, spending some special time with Matt, if you know what I mean." She winked, finally finding her composure.

"All day?" Gia asked.

Carla laughed nervously, twirling a piece of hair around her finger. "Mmhmm. You know us. Just like rabbits!"

"I brought you sandwiches—fresh tomato, basil, and mozzarella." Gia held up the fistful of little sandwich bags, and Carla's eyes lit up. She still needed that sandwich.

"Yes! Come in," Carla told her. "Actually, wait. Uh, just hold on," she said, suddenly appearing nervous. "Wait here a second." Carla closed the door in Gia's face, but through the open window to her side, she could see—and hear—the two of them shuffling things around inside and the hard slam of a laptop closing in a hurry before the door re-opened.

"Come on in!" Carla chirped overly cheerfully as Gia eyed her suspiciously.

"You're being weird. Why are you being weird?"

"I'm not. Let's eat. Giiiiive meeee saaaandwich," she begged Gia, feigning starvation, just as Matt emerged from the hallway, having hidden the computer in an undisclosed location.

He gave a quick wave. "Greetings, neighbor! Ooh, yay, sandwiches! Is this from the garden?"

"Yep. Fresh basil and tomatoes. And the mozzarella is from the farm down by the elementary school," she responded. "Local and organic!"

"Sweet!" Matt grabbed a sandwich bag and pulled apart the zipper seal. He took a bite and started chewing, his eyes closed and head bobbing up and down in satisfaction. "Now that's what I'm talking about. Carla, grab one; it's delicious."

Carla still looked more awkward than usual, but she grabbed a bag and opened it. She wasn't turning down free gourmet sandwiches, even if she *was* feeling guilty for keeping things from her best friend.

"Mmmm, girl. This is to die for, as always," Carla said, agreeing with Matt's assessment of the surprise meal. Suddenly, a glimmer of mischief flashed across Carla's face.

"Hey, you know who I was just thinking about the other day?" she asked, looking directly at Gia.

"Who?" Gia asked through a mouthful of mozzarella.

"Do you remember that guy Benjamin Marshall from years ago? He was kind of nerdy, always showing up at the bars we were at but never saying much to us? He had his own group of friends."

Having just taken a drink from her water bottle, Gia started sputtering, sending droplets of water right toward her friend.

"Ew, Gia... That's gross," Carla said, wiping the water off her face with her sleeve.

"Sorry, I, uh, it went down the wrong pipe."

"So, do you remember Ben?"

"I do," Gia replied simply. "I think he moved to South America or something." She attempted to act nonchalant, but enough emotion was behind Gia's eyes that Carla knew immediately there was more to this story than she let on.

"Why do you bring him up?" Gia asked.

"Oh, I don't know. Just being nostalgic today, I guess. You know? Just thinking about the past and how we've shared so much of our lives," she emphasized the last words, an incognito dig at Gia for keeping whatever had happened between her and Ben to herself.

Matt eyed the two women and thought it was the perfect time to change the subject. He stood up and stretched. "Enough about the past! Let's discuss the present. It's the weekend—patio beers?" He grabbed the remainder of his sandwich, ushering the two women toward the back door.

"Sure," Gia agreed. It wasn't like she had anything else to occupy her time right now, and a bit of a buzz and some friendly chatter might be just what she needed to kick the funk she was beginning to feel without the crutch of online dating to boost her confidence; however fake those compliments were.

Yes, friends. What Gia needed right now was friends. Carla and Gia sat down at the patio table, shielded from the sun by the large umbrella above, as Matt headed back in to grab a cooler full of beer.

"Cheers!" Matt proclaimed.

"To nostalgia," Carla added with a smirk.

Carla raised her beer and clinked it against the other two bottles. They were acting weird, without a doubt, but at least they were good company.

Twenty Questions

GIA

Gia, Carla, and Matt passed the rest of the afternoon and evening on the patio, laughing, drinking, and reminiscing about the past decade that they'd been neighbors—and long before as friends in high school. The conversation flowed freely, and the level of awkwardness was minimal despite the dynamic of three instead of four. Several times, Gia caught Carla and Matt eying each other strangely, but she just chalked it up to lingering flirtation after their all-day "time together" or whatever.

"So, Gia, how's the dating world treating you? Anyone pee in the pool?" Matt asked, chuckling at his own joke. He already knew the answer but did his best to feign ignorance to shift the subject to aid in achieving the desired outcomes of Project Gia.

Gia groaned. "More like pool water tainted with explosive diarrhea! I'm done with it. It's a total disaster. The men only want one thing—and it's not a long, fulfilling relationship, I can tell you that!"

"Nothing wrong with having a little fun here and there," Matt responded, grinning as he elbowed Carla in the ribs. "Am I right?"

Carla rolled her eyes at her husband. "Matty, control yourself. Now is not the time. Our friend and neighbor is going through a rough patch." She threw an arm over Gia's shoulder. "It's our responsibility to be there for her and to help her out... *however we can.*"

Gia couldn't help but wince at how Carla said those last three words. *Something is going on*, she thought—*but what?*

"You're being weird again!" Gia declared.

"No, we're not!" Carla and Matt responded in unison, further compelling Gia to question them.

"What's going on? Tell me. Now."

"Nothing, chicky. Nothing at all. Hey! I have an idea," Gia said, pushing to change the subject. "Let's play a drinking game, like when we were young. Well, young-er, anyway—probably too young to be playing drinking games, actually." Carla squealed in excitement, her eyes lighting up as Gia and Matt looked at her quizzically. It had been years since they'd played a drinking game together. It felt like something from another life-time—one with less responsibility, less heartache, less—just... life.

"Come on!" Carla urged. "It'll be fun!" Matt and Gia nodded their agreement, or at least resignation at Carla, knowing she'd never stop nagging if they didn't play.

"Yay! Okay, I have the perfect game. Just—wait here. I have to get something!" As Carla dashed inside, Matt and Gia stared at each other in confusion.

"Do you have any idea what she's doing?" asked Gia.

"Not a clue, but when it comes to Carla and her crazy ideas, I tend to just let it ride," Matt shrugged, then added, "I'm sure you've learned to do the same by now."

"That I have," Gia said, pushing her long legs out into a stretch as Carla came rushing back to the patio.

"Okay. All set. I have cards and pens!" Carla announced.

Matt stared at her momentarily as if waiting for her to continue, but no additional words came. He sighed. "Carla, I know sometimes you think we are all up there in your mind *with* you—but as it turns out, we aren't. We can't actually hear your thoughts—and we have no idea what you're talking about right now," Matt chuckled.

"Oh! Right! Sorry. We are going to play a rousing game of *Twenty Questions*!"

"Uh, and that's a drinking game? Since when?" Matt asked.

"Since now." Carla passed the pens to Matt and Gia. "Now, each of us gets a pile of these little slips of paper, and we write a question on each. There aren't twenty for each of us. That seemed like overkill, and besides, counting them out was too much work when I'm half in the bag already." She laughed.

"So," Gia started, "questions on the papers. Got it. Where does the drinking part come in?"

"Oh, yeah, so... if you don't answer the question when it's directed at you, you have to take a shot," Carla said nonchalantly.

"A shot? A shot of what?! I was under the impression this was a relaxing patio beer night!" Gia said, placing her hand over her forehead and then massaging her temples.

Carla pulled out a relatively large mixed bag of miniature liquor bottles. "Have these nips left over from the last BBQ. Drinker's choice—or grab bag—whatever you guys want to do."

Gia let out a groan. "Carla, I get my kids back tomorrow. I can't be hungover—that's a nightmare! What happened to simple patio beers?" Gia glanced into the bag of booze.

"Ugh. Whipped cream-flavored vodka. Do you remember how well that went over last time?" she asked.

"If you're referring to the Great Whipped Cream Vodka

Vomit Fest of Senior Year, I do, in fact, recall—and I won't be drinking *any* of that particular type. Never again. That's a vow I'll never break." Carla shook her head from side to side, as if trying to rid herself of any recollection of the night her and Gia had decided to drink an entire bottle of disgustingly sweet cheap vodka at a bonfire party in the woods back in high school. "Just the smell is traumatic to me. But, that night wasn't without its merits! Remember how Matty got us home that night?"

"Oh my GOD—the wagon!" Gia blurted out, nostalgia overtaking her. "He pulled us both home in the wagon because neither of us could walk! And with that said, I ask again: what happened to patio *beers?*"

"Plans change. Live a little. Be spontaneous. Ride the wagon. Play the game. Take the shots. Or... just answer the questions, and you won't have to worry about it." A teasing grin crept across the corners of Carla's lips just as Matt released an unexpected guffaw, finally picking up on Carla's intent for the game. He had to hand it to her; she was a schemer—but she was a very good schemer with a method behind all of her madness.

"Okay, five minutes to write your questions down—begin!" Carla announced, setting a timer on her cell phone.

Realizing that arguing any further would be a lost cause, Gia, Matt, and Carla began furiously writing on the little slips of paper that had been divvied out and set before them.

"Do these have to be PG-rated?" Matt asked, pausing momentarily to wink and nod flirtatiously at Carla.

"Yes, Matt. We can play on our own *another* time." Carla rolled her eyes. "Sorry, Gi. Can't take him anywhere."

"I would like to take this opportunity to respectfully remind you all that this is, in fact, *my* home," Matt chimed in, pretending to be insulted as a grin moved up his cheeks, already rosy from alcohol consumption.

"Yeah, yeah, yeah. Okay, everyone. Get to writing. Time's almost up!" Carla said, pointing at the timer countdown on her phone as everyone again put their pens to paper.

A few moments later, Carla's phone buzzed. "Alright, ladies and gentlemen. It's the moment of truth! It's *Twenty*—or whatever—*Questions* time!"

"Who goes first?" asked Matt.

"Gia answers first... She's the guest, after all. And I ask!" said Carla.

Matt jutted out his lower lip. "Why do *you* get to ask first?"

"Best friend privilege," Carla said, twirling a piece of hair around her finger with a smirk.

"Fine. Whatever. Let's get this show on the road," Matt conceded, knowing Carla was in the midst of hatching a plan in connection with Project Gia.

"Gia, pick a card from my pile. You have to answer the question *honestly* or take a shot. If either of us thinks you're being dishonest... okay, I haven't actually figured that part out yet. We'll cross that bridge if we have to when we come to it. Just pick a card and answer honestly—or chug!"

Gia inhaled deeply and let it out, glancing at the bag of liquor hanging from the arm of Carla's chair. "Lord, here we go," she announced as she pulled a card from Gia's pile. "Do I read this, or do you read it to me?"

"Doesn't matter. You choose," Carla told her.

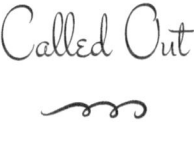

Called Out

GIA

GIA TURNED the card over to reveal the question printed in Carla's messy handwriting. Practically illegible to anyone else, Gia had learned to read her friend's chicken scratch over time thanks to countless notes left in her mailbox, on her door, gate, fence, and so on throughout the years. It was just one of many forms of communication the two had developed over the course of their friendship.

Gia slowly read the words on the card, rolling her eyes as her brain processed them before her mouth could say them out loud:

"What features does your ideal specimen of the opposite sex possess—physical and character traits?"

Carla couldn't help but chuckle at her own question. The

card was *obviously* intended for Gia. If Matt had chosen it, he would have said, "Carla, my love, you are the ideal female specimen!" And, true or untrue, it'd be the best answer he could spout. Gia, however, still had a lot to reveal in this area—and the success of Project Gia depended on it.

While Carla and Matt had completed the bulk of her dating profile on *Only Gardeners*, it was lacking in several areas—and Carla was going to get all those prompts completed tonight or die trying! She also had a few other items on her agenda: one involving a little digging regarding a certain boy named Ben. A blast from the past, perhaps.

"This is a stupid question," Gia began. "You already know what I look for in men. And why do you even care?"

"No, Gia. I know what you wind up *settling* for in men. And I know the red flags you chase like a bull in a damn bull ring. But what are you *actually* looking for? What would make you happy?"

"How is this relevant to the game?" Gia asked, her eyebrows raising.

"It's *Twenty Questions*. It doesn't have to be relevant to anything. That's your question. Answer it or pick your poison." Carla gestured to the bag of booze with a grin, trying to shift the mood to more joyful debauchery.

Resigning herself to the fate of answering the question, Gia gulped a sip of her beer. It wasn't that she felt uncomfortable putting the information into the universe... maybe she could even manifest some happiness by doing so. However, she'd been throwing the question around in her mind for months and still hadn't come up with a very solid list. What *was* she looking for?

"I guess... unmarried," she said with a slight huff, "emotionally available, tall, strong but not a total gym rat, some level of intelligence, a genuine smile, kind eyes, the ability to show affection, honesty, loyalty, a good communicator, someone with similar interests and world view, a desire for self-improvement... I don't know." Gia sighed. "I guess, over and above all, I just want someone who treats me like I matter."

Gia took a deep breath. She hadn't said those words aloud—or even admitted to them in her own mind—but she always knew it deep down. She just wanted someone to make her feel like her existence was worth more than just—being alive. Someone who felt like home. She didn't know how else to describe it. Comfort, love, companionship, shared passions. Something unique and hard to find, with a person who could trigger a feeling she'd caught a brief glimpse of once many years ago.

Unfortunately, mistakes were made on both sides, and it didn't last. It ended before it had barely even had a chance to begin. It was odd that Carla had brought up Ben earlier—no one else had ever known about that, whatever *that* even was.

"That's all I can think of," Gia finished, a tinge of sadness in her voice as the memories of Ben resurfaced, crossing her mind and leaving footprints in their wake. Carla noted the sudden shadow falling over their gathering and quickly changed the subject.

"Okay, great! Good answer. Five stars! You don't have to drink. Now, who is next, me or Matt?" Carla asked, vowing to commit at least part of Gia's answer to memory for the dating profile but curious about why her emotions seemed to take such a sudden turn.

"My turn. I want to answer one of Gia's questions." Matt grinned. Gia chuckled, thinking about the pile of cards in front of her. She shook off the emotional burden of the nostalgia for Ben, what they had, and what could have been. She wanted to escape and head home to process the thoughts that Carla had triggered about what she was looking for—and Ben. It also started her wondering about why Carla had brought Ben up so randomly in the first place. It was a little weird.

As Gia's thoughts began to run away, Matt interrupted the rush by pulling a card from her pile. "Okay, here we go!" he said, his eyes rolling as he began to read the words on the card. "Really,

Gia? Really? This isn't a corporate retreat icebreaker. It's a drinking game between friends!"

Gia cracked a grin, thinking of her questions. "Which one is it? Read it aloud."

Matt's eyes shifted downward again, returning to the card. "If you could be any vegetable, which would you choose and why?"

Upon hearing the question, Carla guffawed, sending beer spewing out of her mouth and across the table toward Gia. "Ew! Carla!" she whined. "That's so gross."

"I'm sorry," Carla began, "but you wrote the question! That is such a ridiculous question." She glanced over at Matt, who appeared to be lost in thought and taking it seriously.

"A potato," he declared with conviction.

"What?" Carla asked.

"I'd be a potato."

The girls giggled. "Okay, it's a two-part question, though. Why, Matthew?" Gia chuckled. "Why would you be a potato?"

"Well... we all know I'm lazy as fuck, right? So, I'd be a couch potato." A groan passed from Carla to Gia. "What?" Matt asked. "It's a pretty damn good answer to a stupid question," he defended.

"Okay, okay. I'll allow it," Gia said, laughing. "Carla's turn!"

Carla glanced at the papers strewn across the table. "Okay, here goes!" Carla said, pulling a paper from Matt's pile and reading it aloud.

"Oooh! Interesting, Matt... If you could ask anyone at this table any question of your choosing, what would it be?" A thoughtful expression crossed Carla's face before she opened her mouth to speak again.

"I would ask Gia about her history with a certain tree-hugging, planet-saving boy named Benjamin."

Carla glanced over at Matt, aware that his intent behind the question was to further the goals for Project Gia by shifting the conversation to a desired topic. He did not, however, expect Carla's question to be quite so direct.

Gia's fingers released their grip on her beer in surprise as the words left Carla's mouth, dropping the drink to the floor where, luckily, it didn't shatter. It did spill all over her feet, though.

"Oh, oops. I, uh, what? What are you talking about?" Gia asked Carla, her face pale as a ghost.

"Gia... Tell me what was up with you and Ben," Carla said. "I thought we told each other everything."

"We did. We do. It's just... it was a long time ago, and it's nothing now. It was nothing then."

"What is nothing? What happened between you two?"

"It's really not anything. I have to go. My feet..." Gia stammered, gesturing to her beer-soaked feet as he rose from her chair. "Uh, raincheck on the rest of the game," she called over her shoulder as she made her way as quickly as possible toward her escape route—the loose board in the fence.

When she was out of view, Carla glanced at Matt. He wasn't smiling.

"What?!" she demanded.

"You know what! That was uncalled for—and far too direct! You knew that wouldn't go well."

"Well, I admit, it didn't go quite as I had hoped." Carla sighed, grabbing one of the tiny liquor bottles from the bag, unscrewing the top, and chugging it before dropping the empty bottle on the table.

She sputtered. "Ew! What was that?" she asked, with a look of horror on her face. Matt reached down and picked the bottle up, holding it in front of his face and grinning as he replied, "Peppermint Schnapps."

"Oh, gross. It tastes like sugar and mouthwash." Carla hated most mint-flavored food and drink. It was typical that she had pulled that particular bottle from such a large stash of alcohol.

"Karma," muttered Matt.

World Corps: Bringing People Together

GIA

As GIA MADE her way through the fence and stumbled across her own yard, she felt buzzed from the alcohol and the revelation that Carla was at least partially aware of the history between her and Ben—well, maybe not aware of the history—but that she knew there *was* history. How did she find out, anyway?

Feeling dazed, she wandered in her back door and headed up the stairs toward her room. Without even thinking, she reached under her bed and pulled out a box. She lifted the lid and glanced inside, eyeing its contents suspiciously as if it had the potential to cause great harm.

"Pandora's Box," she mumbled to herself. "I swore I'd never

go back." Gia reached into the box and grasped a rolled-up paper, unfurling it to read the words to herself.

"Congratulations! You've been accepted as a volunteer in the World Corps program and have been placed in Santarem, Brazil."

She ran her finger over the words. A chance she never took. She turned down an opportunity for an entirely different life out of fear and uncertainty. She remembered the day she had received the letter. It was shortly after Ben had received the very same one, and with each accepted into their first-choice program—Brazil— they would be able to stay together, living out their dreams. At least, that was how it was supposed to play out, but life had other plans.

Gia recalled the rush of sheer joy upon receiving her acceptance letter and placement. All of a sudden, in that moment, life held infinite possibilities for happiness, adventure, and even romance with Ben. The two had gone through school together but ran with different crowds and hadn't had much opportunity to connect during that time. But that all changed quickly after they attended the Information Session for *World Corps*.

Very quickly.

Gia's eyes glazed over as her memories overtook the present moment, bringing a sense of longing and, simultaneously, a stinging pain over dreams long ago shelved and left to die.

"Hey, I know you," a voice came from behind Gia as she waited at the sign-in table for the World Corps info session at the career and opportunity fair held in the community center. Truth be told, she wasn't entirely sure what had triggered her to register for the info session, but something about the idea of spending time traveling and helping the less fortunate pulled at her. She'd spent so much of her life feeling lost and aimless, just doing as she was told, that the idea of truly making a difference was a pretty solid draw for the gap year she'd decided to take after high school.

Even better, World Corps offered a Sustainable Farming volunteer opportunity, where she could truly use her skills and knowledge to have an impact while learning from experts in the field. She was deeply passionate about sustainability, organic farming practices, and integrated pest management, among other garden and farming topics that caused her friends and family to zone out whenever she moved past a cursory explanation.

Gia raised her eyes and turned slightly to see who was speaking from behind. Benjamin Marshall. She knew him, but not well. He was a little nerdy, certainly not from her "clique," but always pleasant when saying hello in passing, and they'd grown up attending the same schools. She rotated to face him.

"Hi there. Learning about World Corps, too?" she asked, a slight shyness in her voice.

"Seems like it could be interesting. Get to see the world, learn about other cultures, do some gardening," Ben said with a comforting smile.

"You garden?" Gia asked, a note of surprise sneaking out with the words. Somehow, she never took him for the gardening, outdoorsy type—always saw him as more of the computer and video gaming type.

"I do, indeed," Ben began. "Been doing it with my dad since before I could walk, pretty much! He's a Master Gardener. I'm close!"

Gia's eyes widened, and her eyebrows moved in an upward motion. "I had no idea!" she added, glancing up to make eye contact with Ben. Until then, she had never noticed the bright specks of green that dotted his light brown eyes, making them sparkle.

"There's a lot about me most people don't know." Ben chuckled. "I'm full of surprises."

"Me too," Gia said. "Most people only ever see what's on the surface." She smiled at Ben, who returned the expression. For a moment, her stomach fluttered, and her heartbeat sped up. Fortunately for Gia, always awkward in the face of new emotions, they were interrupted by an announcement requesting all World Corps Info Session participants to move to the stage area where the presentation would begin.

Gia and Ben followed the crowd to a stage with a podium, screen, and projector. They found two seats beside each other and sat down without saying a word. A few moments later, the screen flashed on, airing the opening scenes of a World Corps volunteer opportunities promotional video. As the video played, neither could turn away from the inspirational footage and perfectly coordinated musical backing. By the film's end, Gia knew she had to do it. She had to be there making a difference, being the change.

"Wow," Ben said as the film concluded. "That was—"

Before he could finish his thought, the director of volunteer opportunities stepped up to the podium and began speaking to the attendees.

"You are all here for a reason. You came together today to learn more about World Corps because you saw an opportunity to make a difference, to be a force for bettering the world, and to work as a unified force across the global community to improve lives, livelihoods, and environments. You recognize that there is the possibility to achieve the greater good, and we offer a way to be a part of that goal—that dream."

Ben and Gia's eyes were glued to the woman on stage, offering promises of a better world achievable through hard work, sharing skills and experience, kindness, compassion, and cultural acceptance. Then, she laid the final straw—gardening and farming.

She spoke of extraordinary worldwide opportunities to change lives, preserve intact ecosystems, and "save the world" through implementing sustainable agriculture in sensitive areas. Another focus was to train locals to use their resources responsibly to generate income without destroying the land for future generations. Gia was hooked. She glanced at the boy beside her and realized he was also drawn to the possibilities.

Gia and Ben sat through the remainder of the presentation, jaws dropping every so often and eyebrows rising as the director detailed exciting goals and outlined the possible avenues to achieve them. Finally, the woman completed her speech, adding that application packets were available to pick up on the way out or could be completed online.

As they stood up, they glanced at each other with wide eyes lit up by the possibility of having a future that mattered.

"Wow," Gia started. "I want to do it!"

"Me too," said Ben, a grin stretching from one cheek to the other. "It sounds amazing."

As far as Gia was concerned, that was the start of Gia and Ben. A shared passion. A commitment to join something more significant than what their small-town life offered. Gia thought back to the time they spent preparing their applications for *World Corps*. After that, they began talking and texting about the program. They soon met daily to work on their essays and discuss the many different placements and opportunities, and the excitement mounted—along with several trickier emotions.

Not only did *World Corps* give them constant subject matter for their little meetings, but they realized just how much they had in common. Ben and Gia were both avid gardeners and relished any opportunity to talk about seed saving, pollinators, and their dream gardens. They began to find comfort in their similarities— a place that felt like home.

Aiden

CARLA

Chapter 11

"MATTY—" Carla started.

"Oh, no, no, no. Don't 'Matty' me," huffed Matt. "You knew that was a dumb thing to do, and you did it anyway. It's like all that matters to you are your little games. This time, you've gone too far. This is your best friend's—who's had an incredibly tough year—feelings. It's just not right."

Carla took a deep breath. It was hard to get Matt angry. He took most of her antics in stride and typically let things roll off his shoulders, but she'd accomplished it with that last question of the night. The one that caused Gia to bolt. He was royally pissed.

"I didn't think she'd leave. I didn't know it would be such a big deal." Carla shifted her gaze to the floor. How was she supposed to know the question about Ben would shake up Gia so bad? All she knew at that moment was that she had to find a way to make it right. Maybe she just needed more information...

As if Matt could sense the gears in her head turning, Matt began to speak again. "Carla, whatever you're thinking about doing, I strongly suggest you let the whole thing go. It's not your place, and your scheming has caused more harm than good. Just drop it. Delete the profile and end it."

Carla knew agreeing with him would be the only way to appease Matt, so she did just that. "You're right, Matty. I shouldn't have gotten involved in this one. I'll take a step back." She worded her concession very carefully, agreeing only to "take a step back," not to become entirely uninvolved—but Matt didn't seem to notice the nuance, giving her a pat on the back, which he quickly shifted into a shoulder rub.

"Good girl," he said, causing a blush to rise up and across her cheeks.

"Matt, you know you can't say those words to me..."

"Oh, I know. And that's why I said them," Matt said, wrapping his arms around her waist and pulling her close. He pressed his lips against hers, pulling her lower lip gently into his mouth. His kiss still caused her to shudder and her knees to weaken, even after years of marriage.

Matt pulled away quickly, giving Carla's hair a firm but gentle tug and whispering in her ear, "Delete the profile," before turning and walking toward the kitchen. Carla groaned.

"You can't just start something like that and then just go along on your merry way!" she called after him.

"Oh, but I just did, though. Delete the profile, and then we'll finish what I started."

Carla huffed. She knew he meant business, and she was too buzzed from their evening on the patio to press the issue. She'd gotten plenty of play time with him earlier in the day, anyway. She could wait. It was time to get down to business.

"Sure, sure. I'll get the laptop..." Carla said, moving toward the bedroom where they had stashed it earlier in the day when Gia had appeared at the door. Instead of bringing the computer out to the kitchen where Matt had begun making a snack, she laid on her side atop the bed, setting it beside her and pulling up the Gardeners Only site. Gia's profile was jam-packed with "likes" and messages at that point, but Carla's curiosity had already been piqued, and she only cared about Gia's—her—interactions with one particular person on the site. Carla clicked on the private message from Ben.

Before focusing on Ben's newest message, she reread the last one she had sent to Ben from Gia's profile, focusing on the last line:

Which part of what happened before you left did you want to discuss?

Then, she shifted her eyes further down to Matt's message.

> *Gia,*
>
> *I'm sorry to hear about your divorce. Is there any way we could talk about things in person? It feels awkward online on a dating site. I promise it's just to talk.*
>
> *Ben*

Carla sighed. Well, that certainly didn't provide any additional information for her to work with. Sure, she could arrange a meeting, but without knowing what had happened between them, she hesitated to do that without Gia's consent. That went even beyond *her* questionable moral compass regarding schemes—especially when they involved her best friend. She also wasn't quite sure Matt would forgive that move under the circumstances, given that she was supposed to be deleting the profile, not arranging a rendezvous between Gia and Ben.

Carla pondered her next move carefully, trying to consider what would be best for Gia, not to mention Carla and Matt's relationship. She decided upon another message...

Dear Ben,

Things are a little crazy right now with work and my kids. Can you tell me what, in particular, you want to talk with me about?

Gia

It was a far cry from the flirting she'd hoped would stem from talking to Ben. She sent the message, hoping it would generate some lead into their past—or give her *something* to help her decide whether to continue down this road or leave the past where it may have belonged. Maybe Ben wasn't even the person she should focus her time on. Perhaps she would be better off responding to—she scrolled her eyes down the page—uh, Mr. Half-Naked Gym Guy on Gia's behalf. *Oh, wait, no. No Gym rats,* Carla thought, remembering Gia's "ideal man" list from their earlier game. As Carla pondered the options, she was startled by a *ding* from the computer. He had responded. Oh! Ben was online!

Gia,

I assumed it would be obvious. I want to talk about Aiden. I've never met him, and I think that needs to change. I'm in a different place in my life, and I realize I've made many mistakes. I want to make them right. Can we please talk in person?

Ben

Carla's eyebrows flew up. Aiden? Aiden was Gia's first-born child... *How could Ben possibly know about Aiden? And, more importantly, why would he want to meet him?* Suddenly, a loud gasp escaped from the depths of her lungs. Matt appeared at the door to check on her just as she said, "Oh my God!"

"Carla, are you okay?" Matt glanced at Carla, who was staring at the computer screen, pale-faced, jaw dropped. "Carla? What's up?" Carla didn't even try to hide the computer screen. She gestured at the laptop with a wave, unable to muster any words. She needed Matt's level-headed guidance and didn't care if he got angry. At this point, she probably deserved it.

Matt walked over to where he could get a better view, sitting beside Carla. He focused on the screen in front of him and began to read. Then, just as Carla's had, his eyes flew open wide.

"Aiden?" he asked. Carla nodded.

"Oh my God, Matt. He looks just like him. We could never figure out who he looked like..." Carla trailed off. Matt nodded. She was right. They had all of the same features. There was no doubting it once the thought settled—Aiden was Ben's child. And Gia had known it all these years and had never told anyone. Carla couldn't decide whether she felt betrayed, hurt, or sad for Gia. How could she have not told her something this important?

As she began processing the situation, her thoughts ran wild, but Matt interrupted her.

"So, we already knew Gia and Steve had only been together a short time when she found out she was pregnant. And that they got married very quickly. Either he never knew he wasn't Aiden's father, or he knew from the jump and chose to raise him as his own, anyhow. I don't think Gia could keep something like that from him. It's not in her nature. And, with that, I think I just developed a newfound respect for her ex-husband! Did they get married to save face?"

Carla shrugged to indicate her uncertainty, still unable to speak any intelligible words. This seemed like a real mess. Only two questions were running through her mind. One: How would she respond to Ben's message? And two: What was she going to tell Gia?

There was no keeping this a secret now. It was about to be blown wide open one way or another.

Remember When

~~~

GIA

GIA PULLED her mind back to the present as she sat on her bed, lifting memory after memory from the box. They hadn't been together long, and it wasn't even an "official" relationship. Yet, somehow, Ben had become the man she measured others against —despite how things had ended.

Gia remembered the day she and Ben had moved unexpectedly from friendship and an unspoken connection to something more. A tear formed in the corner of her eye, but she wiped it away quickly. Everything had gone from magical to a complete disaster in such a short time, but Aiden would never be a regret. Although, he was a constant reminder of what she and Ben once had and lost. Gia pulled a grainy, black-and-white ultrasound photo out of the box—the one she had given to Ben before he departed for Brazil, hoping he would change his mind and stay behind—and her mind began to wander again.

❧

"What do you think Brazil will be like?" Gia questioned, sitting beside Ben on her bed as they thumbed through yet another tourist guide on the Amazon region.

"Magical," Ben said. A smile crossed his face as he glanced up from the book, stopping to take in Gia's excited expression. During the time they'd been planning their volunteer experience with World Corps, they had become inseparable. It was a friend-ship, but also something more—and knowing they would share the experience of Brazil did nothing to curb the longing that had begun to stir within.

Without even thinking, Ben reached over, placed his hand atop Gia's, and gave it a gentle squeeze, catching her eye and smiling as she lifted her head in surprise. She gazed at him quizzi-cally for a moment, then returned his smile. She couldn't help but acknowledge how cute he looked as he awkwardly inched closer, trying to appear as if he wanted a better look at something in the book she held on her lap.

When they were sitting mere inches from each other, Ben placed a hand on Gia's face, turning it to look him directly in the eyes. "Gia, do you feel it?" Ben asked, gazing intently at her.

"Feel what?"

"Nothing. Never mind." Ben's nervousness caught up to him, and he pulled his hand from Gia's, shifted his gaze, and began to rise, catching Gia off guard.

"No, no. Ben. I feel it, too," Gia said, reaching to pull him back. She touched his cheek and gently tugged him toward her until her lips were on his, and all the awkwardness fell away. She pulled away momentarily, saying, "I've felt it for a while now."

"Same," Ben said, finally outwardly revealing the thoughts

circling his mind almost constantly lately. "Gia, you're amazing. You're beautiful. We've become so close so quickly, and I know it's crazy, but I think... I think I might be in love with you."

Gia could feel the warmth enter her face as her cheeks flushed. She was surprised by his words but found she accepted them—and felt the same. She had known it on some level for a while but, unsure of where Ben stood, had been uncertain what to do with those feelings until that moment.

She grabbed his face again, pressing her lips to his, this time more passionately. She pulled back for a moment, only to say, "I love you too, Ben," then returned to the kiss, gripping his lower lip between hers as he took the guide from her lap and tossed it off the bed, placing one hand where the guide had been.

The kiss grew deeper and more desperate, and Ben wrapped his arms around Gia tightly as their breathing deepened, perfectly in synch. Gia leaned in, pressing against him, lost in the warmth and comfort of his body against hers. That had been the most surprising part of all his for Gia. Ben had become her comfort so quickly. She felt at home in his presence and, now, even more so in his arms.

Their tongues danced in perfect rhythm, breathing new life into the emotions that had developed and intensified over the past several weeks as they shared their hopes and dreams for Brazil. Ben pulled away from Gia's mouth and gently turned her head to the side, kissing slowly down her ear and onto her neck, causing her to moan softly as she ran her fingers through his hair.

As he kissed lower on her neck, Ben gently pushed Gia downward onto the bed, trailing his kisses down and across her chest as a hand wandered to her breast, cupping it gently. Gia leaned upward to sit up again for a moment, lifting her shirt over her head and tossing it aside, inviting him to continue. Ben reached behind her back and began to fiddle with her bra clasp until Gia reached behind to help, noting how sweet it was that he wasn't already a bra strap expert.

Ben pulled the garment away from her body, tossed it aside,

and began kissing downward until he reached her nipple. He wrapped his lips around it softly, teasing gently with his teeth, eliciting a low moan from Gia.

"Are you okay?" he asked, concern written across his face. "Is this okay?"

"More than okay. Don't stop," Gia breathed. "Please don't stop."

"Gia... you're perfect," Ben said quietly before returning to explore her body further.

Gia blushed. She was never great at taking compliments, but she could tell Ben was being sincere. As his mouth traveled across her body to her other breast, his hand trailed downward until it rested on her inner thigh. She could tell he was nervous to go further, but she needed him to be touching her. Still wearing her jeans, she grabbed his hand and positioned it between her legs, raising her hips to move her body against his hand.

"Ben," Gia said quietly, "I want you." She traced her fingers down his abdomen, landing on his belt buckle and fiddling with it until she could pull it open.

Ben groaned. "I want you, too. So badly."

"Then, I'm yours," Gia said, gazing up at him as she undid the zipper on his jeans and tugged at them, indicating her intent.

"Are you sure?"

"More than anything."

Ben kicked off his shoes and removed his pants, then reached forward to undo the button and zipper on Gia's, one hand still resting between her legs. Ben relocated his hand to grip the waistline of her pants and guided them down her legs and off as she wrapped her fingers around his cock. It was bigger than she had expected. For some reason, she hadn't envisioned the somewhat nerdy Ben being so well-endowed.

Ben groaned. "Gia, you feel so good." He moved her hand off him and placed it firmly on the bed. "I need to taste you." Ben kissed his way down Gia's torso and abdomen, coming to rest between her legs and licking the length of her slit. His tongue found her clit and began sucking and nibbling her most sensitive part, causing Gia to raise her hips in response to the stimulation, pushing his face against her body.

"You taste so fucking good," Ben said, lifting his head.

"You feel so good, Ben. I want you. I want you inside me. Now."

"Now?" asked Ben.

"Right now. Immediately."

"I don't have a—"

"I don't care. Be inside me, Ben. Please?"

Ben let out a growl and placed his legs on either side of Gia, grabbing her head and kissing her passionately.

"Are you—"

"Ben, please, please, just do it. I want to feel you inside me. I want you in me... now. Right now."

Hearing that, Ben guided himself inside Gia, pushing slowly to fill her, then gaining speed and intensity as they rocked together. Gia matched his rhythm with her hips, raising them to meet each thrust, wrapping her legs around him tightly to try to bring him even closer to her. She felt like she couldn't ever be near enough. It wasn't possible.

She gripped at any body part she could get her hands on, arms, wrists, hands, taking him in, relishing the sensation of her skin against his. Gia was surprised at how muscular Ben was under his clothing. How had she never noticed how incredible his body was?

Ben grabbed Gia's arms and pinned them behind her, kissing her passionately. Gia's thighs began to shudder as they rose, and her breathing quickened as Ben increased the speed of his thrusts. "It feels like you're close, baby. I'm close too," Ben whispered into her ear, sending her right over the edge. She was big on pet names, and hearing Ben call her "baby" was more than she could handle.

"Ben, fill me. I want you to fill me. Please?" Gia said, knowing she was on the edge. As the words left her lips, her hips rose, and the waves of an intense orgasm swept over her. As her climax hit, a surge of emotions came right along with it. How had this even happened? She clung to Ben as if for dear life as he let out a deep, low-pitched groan—guttural and sexy—and exploded within her, wrapping his arms around her body and holding her close.

They collapsed onto each other, clinging tightly to one another as if trying to hang onto everything that had just happened, afraid that if they moved, it would all disappear—the feelings and the events leading to that moment. A deep fear hung over them that if they were to let go, things would return to the way they had been before.

It wasn't her first time, but something about the way that Ben seemed to appreciate every inch of her body and her mind made it feel brand new—something about how he cared whether she was "okay."

"Ben," Gia stammered. "I do love you."

"I love you, too."

The Dating Game

CARLA

Chapter 13

"CARLA, we have to talk to her," Matt told his wife. "We—you —can't keep talking to him like this. He thinks he's talking to the mother of his child he's never even met!"

Carla sighed and closed the laptop. "You're right. I know. You're completely right. We just have to figure out how to bring up the subject with her..."

"Carla, I think in this particular instance, being straightforward and honest is your best option."

"But then she'll ask me how I know about Aiden!"

"And you'll tell her exactly what you did—and that you had her best interest at heart." Matt rolled his eyes. "The way I see it, you don't have many options. This is their lives we're talking about—their kid. It isn't your place to be involved at all, but since you've managed to put yourself right in the middle, yet again, you've got to tell her everything."

Carla nodded her agreement, dreading the conversation with Gia that would inevitably follow. Matt grabbed her cell phone from the nightstand, tossing it toward her. It landed on the bed beside Carla, and she reached for it, groaning.

"Can't this wait until tomorrow? We're all a little buzzed, still. Let's just shut the computer down and deal with this in the morning when we are thinking clearly," Carla begged.

"Do you promise you'll call or go over there first thing in the morning?"

"I promise."

"Fine. Go to bed," Matt ordered.

Carla reached for the laptop. "But I just want to—"

"NOW!"

Carla sighed. "Fine," she said. "Will you tuck me in, Matty?" she added softly, moving her lips into the pout she knew he couldn't resist.

"Yes... but I'm taking the computer out of here when I leave." He chuckled. "You can't be trusted with technology—or anyone's personal life, for that matter!"

Carla scrunched up her nose, acting offended, but wiggled her way to the top of the bed as Matt pulled the covers down and lifted them over her.

"Goodnight, you little chaos bringer, you. Tomorrow's another day. You can wreak more havoc then."

"I love you, Matty. I'm sorry."

"Don't be sorry to me." He raised his hands in a show of impartiality. "Tell it to the judge," he gestured to the house next door—Gia's house. "I love you, too." Matt gave her a peck on the forehead and walked to the door, flipping the light off on his way out. He was almost into the hallway when he realized he was empty-handed, turned on his heel, and returned to Carla's bedside.

"Almost forgot," he said, grabbing the still-closed laptop and tucking it under his arm before walking out again.

"You have no faith in me, Mr. Matty."

"After your shenanigans tonight, nope! Sweet dreams, princess."

With that, Matt left. He walked into the living room, stopping momentarily to glance at the computer and rubbed his chin thoughtfully. "I wonder," he said aloud to himself. "No, I shouldn't," he answered his own question.

He wouldn't get involved. Carla had done enough already. Matt set the computer on the coffee table, moving into the kitchen, where he poured another drink before returning and sitting on the couch.

Matt turned on the TV and began channel surfing, searching for something to watch.

"Boring, lame, stupid," he muttered as he flipped through channel after channel of shows that did nothing to spark his interest. Then, his gaze shifted again to the computer resting on the table before him.

He had an idea. It didn't involve Gia—at least not entirely— so he didn't think it would lead to any more trouble than Carla and he were already in. It would just help them get a better handle on who Ben was and, perhaps, his intentions for being back in the area—just a little detective work. No harm, no foul.

Matt opened the laptop computer, which remained logged into "Gia's" *Only Gardeners* account. No new messages since the last, and he had vowed he wouldn't do anything further under the guise of Gia, so he logged out, then moved the cursor to the "New Account" screen and got to work creating a phony profile using stock photos of a pretty female in a vegetable garden. *It's incredible how easy it is to find what you need when you need it on the internet these days,* he thought.

Matt guessed what he was doing fell under the heading of "catfishing" and that the profile would probably be flagged and deleted by the admins relatively soon—but he didn't need much time. From memory, he set the search parameters on the phony profile to the local area and entered the information he recalled from Ben's profile, hoping it would pull him up without too much hassle. Sure enough, Ben's image appeared on his screen after swiping left on several profiles. Fortunately, *Only Gardeners* wasn't exactly *the* most popular dating site out there, which made it significantly easier to find!

Boom. Immediate right swipe. "We're in business," he said aloud. "Now... let's just wait and see if Mr. Benjamin is interested in getting to know, uh—" Matt glanced at the top of "his" profile before finishing his sentence with his chosen name, "Marianna." He leaned back and rested his feet on the coffee table, his arms behind his head. Before long, his eyelids were heavy, and his head began to nod to one side until he began to snore.

"MATT!" The voice rang in his ears, waking Matt up from a deep sleep. His eyes shot open in shock and confusion. He saw Carla standing beside him, arms resting on her hips. *Oh no,* he thought. *Her angry pose. What'd I do?* Carla gestured at the computer on the coffee table with wild hands.

"*Who,* exactly, is MARIANNA? Are you on a dating site?!" Carla's nostrils flared angrily, and her eyebrows were raised, arching downward, making her face look menacing.

"What are you talking—oooh!" As his memory slowly returned to him, he began to chuckle. Carla thought he was browsing *Only Gardeners* for himself, he realized.

"Why are you laughing? What could you possibly be laughing about at a time like this, when our marriage is shaking precariously on its last legs, and you're looking for someone to take my place!" Carla's hands moved frantically, and it only upset her more to see the calm, bemused look on Matt's face. "What?!" she roared.

"You, my love, are being crazy. I'm Marianna. Marianna is me." A look of confusion took hold of Carla's facial expression until it was suddenly replaced by one of understanding.

"Matt! You can't perform covert operations *without* me! What the hell!?"

"You were asleep!"

"Because you told me I had to!"

"I got bored," Matt said. "And I felt like I could get some information that may be helpful—but then I fell asleep, I guess—until you so rudely awakened me with accusations of infidelity. I can't even handle one woman! Why on earth would I want another?" He scoffed at Carla, who returned the look by sticking out her tongue. They stared at each other before Matt finally broke the silence.

"Joint covert operations, then?"

Carla nodded, feeling slightly silly about how she had acted—once again.

"But first, breakfast. My treat!"

"You're cooking?" Matt glanced at Carla incredulously, surprised she was offering to prepare a meal of her own free will.

"Heck no. The diner down the street delivers now. We can see if Ben responded to your swipe while we wait for it to arrive, then devise a plan! I need eggs with corned beef hash and a massive cup of coffee before my brain will work."

"Aren't you supposed to be calling Gia to talk 'first thing this morning'?"

"Hash. Eggs. Coffee. No coffee, no talky. Anyway, she doesn't have the kids this morning—she will want to get some extra sleep time in."

"Whatever you say. Call in the order." He waved a hand toward Carla's cell phone and leaned back against the couch, returning to the position he had been in before he was so rudely interrupted. "We ride at dawn!"

"What? Why are you so weird?" Carla asked, glancing at him.

"I don't know. You seem to like it," Matt said with a shrug as he wrapped an arm around Carla's waist and pulled her close.

We Need to Talk

CARLA

IT DIDN'T TAKE LONG for breakfast to arrive, and Carla and Matt didn't hesitate for a moment. Carla ran to the door, turned both the top lock and the smaller one on the doorknob, and pulled it open. She used one foot to keep it propped open while she reached down to grab the food the delivery person had left on the front step, as instructed on the app. *Getting food has become far too easy. I'm gonna have to start watching my figure,* thought Carla as she lifted the bag and carried it inside.

"Food!" she announced loudly, beckoning for Matt to join her in the kitchen. He had disappeared into the bedroom a few minutes ago, likely to lie down and nurse his slight hangover before the greasy breakfast arrived. He quickly emerged at the promise of eggs and hash, walking over to the kitchen table where Carla pulled takeout containers out of a bag. He plopped down and joined her in opening them.

"I'm starving," he declared, reaching his arms up over his head in a stretch.

"Me too... but eat fast! We have things to do!"

"Like, for example, going to the next-door neighbor's house to explain to your best friend why you may have just invited a healthy—perhaps unhealthy—dose of chaos into her life?"

"Matt, I will. Right after we go online and see what's going on with our—I mean, Marianna's—profile."

Matt rolled his eyes, and Carla rolled hers back even harder. "Where'd you get that name, anyway? Mariannnnna," Carla emphasized the 'n,' drawing it out longer than the rest of the word. Even though the profile was fake, she couldn't help being mildly offended by the stock photos Matt had selected to encompass the role of this beautiful temptress, none of which resembled Carla in the slightest!

"I have no idea," Matt said. "Must have been on the TV or just popped into my mind or something. Anyway, let's eat!"

"...She's not even that pretty," Carla added as she divvyied up the food items from the bag and handed Matt the plastic cutlery the diner provided. Realizing that Matt was refusing to take the bait and have an argument over a fictional dating profile, Carla took a bite of her toast. She knew she was mostly upset over her rapidly approaching, and utterly unavoidable, meeting with Gia. They ate quickly, and conversation was minimal as each pondered what they'd find when they opened the laptop on the other side of the room.

Carla was torn. Part of her wanted the meal to be over and done as quickly as possible so she could get online. She also knew that the sooner that happened, the sooner she would have to head over to Gia's and confess her sins. It had to be done, but she had absolutely no idea how Carla would respond, given that she still hadn't figured out the true nature of her and Ben's history. *What were they to each other? Why didn't she tell me?*

Carla felt hurt that such a seemingly critical component of her supposed best friend and long-time neighbor's life had been kept from her—but, at the same time, recognized that maybe there was a reason for it. Given Carla's online antics over the past several days, it was entirely understandable that Gia would keep something so potentially complicated a secret—probably to keep Carla from getting involved!

As Matt finished his last bite, he rose and began to clear the table.

"Do it later," Carla begged. "Can you do it while I'm over at Gia's, Matty? Please? Let's get to the computer... please?" Carla's lower lip jutted out and folded over slightly, pouting.

"You're ridiculous," Matt said with another eye roll. "But, in this case, fine. Get the computer."

Carla threw her chair back, almost falling out of it in the process as she rose quickly. She practically skipped to the other side of the room, ignoring the pounding in her head from one—or a few—too many drinks the night before. Carla grabbed the laptop and opened it up, logging onto the home screen. There it was, *Only Gardeners*—and Marianna. Unfortunately, despite a multitude of 'likes' for the fake profile, there were no actual matches.

"Ben didn't like us—Marianna—back?" Carla looked appalled.

"Maybe he only has eyes for Gia now," Matt chuckled. "Or maybe he hasn't been online since last night. I doubt he lives on the dating site."

"If he's waiting for a response from her, he should!" Carla declared, standing up for her best friend's interest even without knowing where her best interest truly stood. *Is Ben a friend or foe?*

"Okay, my favorite little meddler. It's time for you to go do your dirty work. Or confess to your dirty deeds, anyway. Trot on over to Gia's like you promised. We can check again later, depending on how things go between you and her."

Carla let out a groan. "This is the worst day *ever*. I don't want to!"

"Then, you shouldn't have dug the hole. Maybe you should bring her, like, a peace offering or something..." Matt suggested.

Carla rubbed her chin thoughtfully for a moment, considering the suggestion.

"Hmm. Not a bad idea. What, though?" Carla's gaze wandered across the room, searching for inspiration. It lingered on the relatively well-stocked wine rack, but she shook her head after a moment. *No, no wine. She's probably hungover. I know I am.* She continued to scan the room. *Nothing, nothing, nothing, Bingo!*

Sitting on top of the wall unit—in the same place she'd thrown it over two weeks ago—was the gift certificate she'd received to dine at the newest restaurant in town. *Charm to Table* served 100% local, seasonal, gourmet small farm-to-table fare. Carla knew from the moment she saw it that she'd probably never use it. She and Matt were more of a wings-and-beer-type couple, but since it had been an anniversary gift, she held on to it. Gia, however, with her love for fresh garden produce and growing things in general, would *love* it. It was right up her alley.

"Matt! *Charmed to Table!*"

"Huh?" Matt looked up and glanced over at Carla, confused.

"I'll bring her the gift certificate to the new restaurant—the one my mom gave us for our anniversary. It'll make her happy, and you and I will never use it together, anyway. She and I could go... or, depending on how the conversation goes today, we can set her and Ben up to reunite!"

"For the love of all things good in the world, woman!" Matt began. "Leave the poor girl alone and let her find peace far away from your meddling! Take the certificate, give it to her, make amends for what you've done, and go out to eat with her. The end. Whatever happens—or doesn't—between Gia and Ben is her business, *not yours*. Or mine, for that matter," he finished, glancing at the dating profile he'd created on the computer screen with a guilty expression.

Carla winced. He only called her "woman" when he was truly shocked at her behavior, which didn't happen very often, given her track record. She sighed and nodded, signaling to Matt that she recognized he was right, and that she'd behave.

"Okay, okay. I get it. I'm going over there now." Carla took a deep breath and started for the back door, hoping Gia was already outside in the garden. This was a conversation she'd prefer to have in the place where she knew her friend felt most comfortable— *Gia's happy place.*

As she got closer to the fence and moved the loose post to enter Gia's backyard, she pressed her face into the empty space it left, eyeing the garden area. She didn't see anyone initially, but she'd learned after years of entering this way that it meant nothing. More often than not, Gia would pop up from somewhere between the raised beds, covered in dirt, holding a garden tool or a piece of produce like a trophy.

Feeling a little more awkward than usual this time, given the unknown outcome of the conversation they would be having, Carla didn't simply slip through the fence and enter. Instead, she called out to her friend, making her presence known beforehand.

"Gia? Are you out here?" Carla questioned.

"Hey, Carla. I'm in here!" Gia's voice rang out from the largest fenced area of the garden, which housed several varieties of lettuce, spinach, kale, arugula, and various other salad greens. Carla glanced over and saw the wide-brimmed gardening hat bouncing up and down with her movements as Gia hand-plucked weeds from between the heads of lettuce.

"So many freaking weeds this year!" Gia complained. "I can barely keep up! I need to hire a second gardener!"

"*Only Gardeners*-dotcom?" Carla responded, hoping it would come off as a light-hearted joke that would also get the discussion they needed to have rolling.

"Ha! Never again. No more dating. Online or anywhere else!" Gia scoffed.

"Uh... so, Gia... would you say you're in a good mood today?" Carla's eyes were open wide, making her appear more like a deer-in-the-headlights than a friendly neighbor and Gia's best friend.

"I was. Now, I'm not so sure. Carla, what's up? Should I sit down for this?"

"That might be best."

"Oh, Lord. Here we go," Gia grumbled, raising her eyes to the sky in pre-mature exasperation.

The Truth Hurts

GIA

FROM THE MOMENT her friend entered the yard, Gia could tell that it wasn't just for a typical weekend visit comprised of drinking wine, laughing, and eating snacks. When Carla told her to sit down, she didn't even question it. Gia needed a break, anyway. She had been out in the garden since the sun began to rise, pulling weeds and harvesting herbs. She hadn't slept much the night before as images and memories of Ben kept sneaking into her thoughts. *Why did Carla have to bring him up, anyway?*

As they settled into a seated position on the edge of the closest raised garden bed, Gia noticed Carla fidgeting with something in her hands.

"I brought you something!" Carla started in a tone of false enthusiasm as she realized where Gia's eyes had fallen.

"What is it? And for what?"

"Oh, just because! Can't one neighborhood girl bring a gift to another as a kind gesture in the spirit of friendship?" Carla shoved the gift certificate to *Charmed to Table* in Gia's direction. "It's to the new farm-to-table in town. I thought we could go. Or you could go with someone else, maybe."

Gia took the gift certificate and turned it over a few times. "Valid for one 5-course prix fixe meal for two," she read aloud.

"It's their grand opening offer. To get people in to try it out," Carla explained.

Gia tucked the card into her pocket, fully aware that it was probably an anniversary gift that had been given to her and Matt that they had no plans to use. "It sounds great, but do you want to tell me why you're *really* here now? I know you didn't traipse over here to give me a gift that's been sitting on your wall unit for weeks."

"Oh, you saw it there? Well, anyway, you'll get better use from it than we will. It's not really our thing," Carla added, justifying giving it to Gia.

"So... Would you like to tell me why you're here and acting weird now?"

Not really, but I don't think I have much of a choice in the matter." Carla pushed a piece of hair away from her face, revealing a concerned look that spread across her features.

"How bad is this, Carla?" Gia asked, hoping whatever it was she had done this time wouldn't have any significant impact on her daily life. It certainly wouldn't be the first time Carla had stuck her nose where it didn't belong!

"So, that's the thing..." Carla began, shifting position, clearly uncomfortable with the discussion.

"What's *the thing*, exactly?"

"I'm not sure how bad the repercussions will be—but I am deeply, sincerely, one hundred percent sorry for my actions!"

The pleading undertone in Carla's voice made Gia's stomach churn.

"Carla, what actions? You're scaring me. Start from the beginning. What's going on? What's up?"

"Well... okay. So, remember the other day when you said you didn't want to date anymore?"

"Yeah, and that remains the case. Go on."

"Well, I started thinking that maybe you *should* date, but that you just weren't looking in the right places or something, so I decided, well, I figured I'd look *for* you. I only wanted to help."

"What do you mean?" Gia said. "Look how? Like, find someone to set me up with? You've done that countless times already! What's the big deal, Carla? What's different?"

Carla's eyes shifted to the ground. It wasn't a good sign when Gia started or finished a sentence with her name.

"I kind of sort of made you a dating profile on *Only Gardeners*. I thought—"

"You *what?*" Gia interrupted. "After you knew how I felt about dating, and men, and the whole damn thing? You decided you'd just ignore all that and make a dating profile for me? So, what? Did you actually pretend to *be* me? Did you talk to men as me? Carla! How far did this go?"

Carla stared at a patch of lavender just beginning to flower as she avoided Gia's gaze. She plucked a piece and crushed it between her fingers, hoping its sweet, floral scent would calm her. Gia was always saying the scent of lavender was aromatherapeutic, and that it could bring a sense of peace and tranquility. Somehow, Carla doubted it would work in this case, but she figured it couldn't hurt, either.

"Well, the good news is, you're a hot commodity. Every single romantically unattached male gardener in the tri-state area seems interested in your profile!"

Gia rolled her eyes. "I told you. I don't want to date. Wait, if that's the good news, that means—is there more bad news here— beyond you impersonating me on the internet, of course?"

Carla paused. Gia sucked in a deep breath of air, held it a moment, then released. "Maybe. Matt and I know about Aiden. We know about Ben." She braced herself for Gia's response, unsure whether it would come in the form of anger, sadness, or relief.

In fact, once the words escaped Carla's mouth, Gia was oddly calm, as if she knew it had only been a matter of time before someone learned the truth.

"... How did you find out?"

"He reached out to you—well, me—on *Only Gardeners.* He's back."

"What do you mean he's back? How could he be back? He's in Brazil. Is he visiting his parents?"

"He's not. He's here to stay, I think. And he wants to see you. I'm pretty sure he wants to meet Aiden."

The calm façade originally painted onto Gia's features faded into a look of panic. "He can't. He shouldn't. Carla, this is a disaster! Aiden doesn't even know he exists!" Gia paced the narrow garden path in between the raised beds. She lifted both hands and placed them against her face, groaning into them.

"How did this even happen?"

"Well, he swiped right." She shrugged. "Then, messaged you —well, me, I guess, and Matt."

"Matt is involved? How'd you pull that off? He's usually the voice of reason!"

"I know, it's crazy, right?"

"Okay, let's stay on topic here. What did Ben tell you? What did he say *exactly?*"

"I mean, brief recap, not a whole lot. He said he just wants to talk about what happened before he left and about Aiden—in person."

Gia groaned again, knowing she wouldn't be able to see Ben face-to-face without breaking down. She still held on to so much emotion about their situation. They may have been old wounds, but she knew the very sight of him would be enough to send her into a downward spiral, especially after all that had happened over the past year. She was finally piecing her life back together after her divorce, and now this.

In the back of her mind, however, she couldn't help but wonder if, perhaps, this was some sort of 'one that got away...' fate stirring the pot just as her life began to settle down. Gia pushed the thought out of her mind, trying to think about the situation calmly and rationally.

"Give me the login info," Gia blurted out.

"What?"

"The account name and password for *Only Gardeners*. I need to see for myself. I have to know what was said before I decide what to do about this."

Carla nodded slowly. "Okay. That's fair. Do you want to sit together and go through everything so you can yell at me in person?"

"No. I need to do this alone. Here." Gia opened the notepad feature on her cell phone and shoved it toward Carla. "Enter it here. Then, I need to go inside to think."

Carla shot Gia a funny look. Gia chuckled, recognizing how strange that sounded coming from her. The garden was usually where she most effectively pondered her life, but now she just wanted to escape it. It made her think of her shared interests with Ben. Gia had a feeling she'd be getting enough reminders of that time in her life soon. It made her want to escape the garden, which now felt like it was closing in on her, stealing her breath.

Gia held a hand against her cheek, feeling its warmth. She always got hot when her emotions were high, and this was absolutely one of those moments. Carla handed her phone back with the stored login information. "Are you sure you don't want me to stay?" she asked, squeezing her friend's hand.

"No. Not this time, but thanks."

"Are you mad at me?"

"Carla, I'm not mad. This secret was bound to come out eventually. I just wish you'd mind your own damn business sometimes." Despite the emotional turmoil simmering below the surface, Gia's voice had taken a slightly more playful tone.

"But, if I did that, I wouldn't be me. And you love me. Right? Tell me you looooove me," Carla said, teasing, but also desperately needing to hear it from her best friend.

"Yes, you crazy meddling nuisance. I love you. Now, let me go handle some business."

"What are you going to say to him?"

"I have no idea."

"Remember the gift card! Maybe you two can meet there to talk?"

"That sounds more like a date than a meeting with the father of my first child—the one he left behind to hug trees in the fucking Amazon rainforest."

Carla shrugged. "It was worth a try. Maybe eventually?"

"Don't bet on it. Ben left me once. I'm not giving him the option to do it again." Gia scoffed. "Now, run along. Oh, and tell Matt he's no longer considered as the voice of reason for the two of you. And you're both still in trouble—I'll figure out your punishment later."

Carla wrapped her arms around Gia, pulling her close. "I'm sorry," she whispered. "I won't do anything like this ever again." The words elicited a slight chuckle from Gia.

"I'll believe *that* when I see it."

Carla rose and ran toward the gap in the fence, excited to tell Matt that the interaction had gone much better than she'd expected. As far as she could tell, she still had a best friend living next door. She hoped that would remain the case after Gia spoke with Ben—and saw the dating profile Carla had created.

Positive

GIA

Chapter 16

GIA CLENCHED the cell phone in her hand as she made her way back toward her house. The login information to the dating site could potentially change her life and that of her child—her entire family dynamic, really. Aiden had been conceived during her and Ben's brief but passionate love affair. For two young kids just out of high school barely getting to know one another, the news of the pregnancy came as a surprise at best.

Gia entered the living room and sat on the recliner, opening the footrest portion and stretching her legs. She held her phone against her chest and closed her eyes momentarily, remembering the day her life changed in ways she had never imagined possible.

❦

Gia held the pregnancy test between her fingers, jaw dropped and eyes wide. "How could this happen?" she muttered to herself, bringing her hands to her face and resting them against her cheeks, hot to the touch. Tears formed in the corners of her eyes until she could no longer hold them back, and they streamed down her face in torrents. Gia knew exactly how it had happened, but it was just that one time without protection. The first time.

She had been feeling ill for several weeks, lethargic, exhausted, and constantly nauseous, especially when she forgot to eat. Finally, it clicked in her mind, and she'd purchased the home pregnancy test without telling a soul. It would be negative, anyway. It had to be, she remembered thinking. However, as she sat there awaiting the results, it turned out it was not.

Positive.

Gia was pregnant.

She managed to get from the bathroom to her bedroom unnoticed by her mother, who was downstairs in the kitchen preparing dinner. She climbed into her bed, curled up into a ball and clenched her arms around her legs. The tears became unstoppable then. Torrents of regret poured down her face. She loved Ben, but how could she tell him about this? Their plans certainly didn't include a baby! They were supposed to join World Corps, travel to Brazil, and embark upon the adventure of their lives—a pregnancy just didn't fit the plan.

After her tears had stopped—at least for the time being—Gia reached for the phone near the side of her bed. She picked it up and dialed Ben's number, holding her breath while waiting for him to answer.

"Hello?"

"Hey, Ben. It's Gia."

"Hey, you! What's up? Why does your voice sound funny? Are you okay?"

"Uh," Gia hesitated, unsure if this was the type of information one supplied over the phone. "I'm not really, but I need to see you in person. Can you come over?"

"... I don't like the way this sounds. Are you breaking up with me?"

"I, uh, no. I mean, I didn't even know we were officially together."

"Well, I guess we never really talked about it. But, if you want to end things, can you just tell me now and save me the trip there?"

"Ben... That's not it. I really need you to come over," Gia said, her voice hitching as the words came out. "Please?"

"Okay, as long as that's not what you're going to tell me, I'll be right there. Do you need anything on my way?"

"No, I'm okay. Just hurry, please." Gia's voice sounded shaky, and Ben must have noticed the urgency.

"Okay, I'm on my way right now. No stops. Hang tight."

The time between hanging up the phone and Ben's arrival was only minutes, but to Gia, it felt like hours. She felt paralyzed, unable to move, incapable of rational thought. Straightening up her posture and wiping the tears from her swollen eyes, she regained her composure for a moment.

"Mom?" Gia yelled.

"Mmmhmm?" her mother called back, her mouth clearly occupied with tasting some part of what would be dinner.

"Ben's coming over for a little bit. Can you just tell him to come up? I'm in the middle of some Brazil research," she lied.

"Of course. Is he staying for dinner? There's plenty!"

"Uhm, I—I'm not sure. I don't think so."

"Okay, make sure to invite him. I like Ben. He's such a nice boy. Smart, too."

"I will. Just send him up, okay?"

"Okie dokie!"

A few minutes later, Gia heard Ben's car pull up. She glanced out her bedroom window to see him parking at the curb in front of her room. She watched as he walked from the car to the front of her house, a look of concern in his expression Gia hadn't yet seen from him. When they were together, they were usually planning out their exciting future, not dealing with surprise teenage pregnancy. She could only imagine how he would react when he learned about their... situation.

Gia heard the doorbell ring, and her mom answered it, exchanging a few pleasantries with Ben before directing him to Gia's room. Three gentle knocks at her closed door told her he had made it. "Come in," Gia told him. "It's unlocked."

The door handle turned, and Ben appeared, ducking his head into the doorway before the rest of his body followed. He looked so young to Gia today. So unprepared for the news she was about to throw at him.

"Is everything okay? What's going on? You sounded upset on the phone." Ben walked over to Gia's bed and gazed into her eyes, trying to ascertain the reason behind her strange mood.

"I... I'm not okay. I don't know what to do. How could this happen?" Gia brought her hands to her face and cradled it, covering her eyes to avoid looking at Ben. It was clear from their puffy redness that she had already been crying.

"How could what happen, Gia?" Ben's eyebrows were furrowed in concern and confusion. He sat beside her and placed a hand on her knee. "What's going on?" he asked, his voice soft and comforting but worried. Before Gia could respond, Ben's expression shifted to one of surprise and panic as his eyes caught the pregnancy test resting on the nightstand beside the bed. Taking note of the + symbol, Ben shook his head a few times as the meaning of the symbol sunk in. "You?" he asked, sounding terrified. Gia nodded. "Me?" Ben questioned. She nodded again.

"Who else? It's only been you. It's only ever been you."

Ben gave her a look that showed her he already knew. He trusted her. "I know," he confirmed once he could find the words. "What—what do we do?" Ben asked the question, but no words came. He didn't wait for a response or ask again. Instead, he reached his arms around Gia, pulled her down onto the bed so they were lying down, and hugged her close to provide comfort. They remained that way for several minutes, letting the news sink in and silently processing it.

Finally, Gia interrupted the silence. "I want to keep it."

"What?" Ben said, his expression unreadable.

"I want to have the baby, and I want to keep it. It's part of me. It's part of us." Gia touched her stomach. While there were no external changes to her body, she imagined that inside, there was a part of her and Ben growing with each passing day.

"What about Brazil?" Ben asked. Gia didn't fault him for the insensitive question at that moment. She knew it had to be asked. That was their plan. It had been Ben's plan even before he and Gia had grown close. She knew that from the second he'd accepted the volunteer position at World Corps, it was never optional. There was never any question. It was the next step in his life—the step that would get him out of this small town where he'd spent his whole life. He had made it clear that he saw it as his only escape and Gia worried that this would seem like some sort of trap that had been set to hold him back from his future.

"Maybe Brazil can wait, maybe—I don't know. Maybe when we're older, we can—"

"Gia," Ben interrupted. "You said so yourself; we weren't even officially together. I don't know what any of this means. But I can't give up Brazil—not for you, not for a kid I don't even know."

"Your kid. Our kid."

"I need time to think," Ben countered. "This is a lot. This is just—it's a lot."

Gia nodded, trying to appear understanding, but feeling as if she could break apart into tiny pieces. None of this was easy for her, and she knew it couldn't be for him, either. Fighting off the urge to burst into sobs, she merely said, "I get it. We can talk later."

Ben threw his legs around to the side of the bed and rose to his feet. Gia could see tears forming in the corners of his eyes as he kissed her on the forehead, and she could tell he was trying to hold them back. She had already had her first cry over this; it was his turn, and she could tell Ben wanted to be alone. He deserved that, at least.

Ben squeezed her hand, whispered, "I'm sorry," and walked out her bedroom door.

A Distraction

~~~

GIA

Chapter 17

Snapping back to the present, Gia lifted the phone and gazed at the notepad application that housed the login information for *Only Gardeners*. She rolled her eyes. *Seriously?*

Account Name: DirtyHoe39
Password: GiaDates12345*

Original. With a screen name like Dirty Hoe, was it any surprise that the men were running to her profile in droves? Gia knew it was a play on words—a garden hoe, not a skanky ho—but, just the same, she made an internal note to yell at Carla for it later. She took a deep breath, held it for ten seconds, and released it through her mouth. She'd been working on deep breathing techniques for several months, trying to reduce her stress and remain calm during trying moments—single parenting was hard!

Gia clicked into the app store on her phone and searched for *Only Gardeners,* quickly finding it. "Here we go," she said as the application began downloading. When a prompt popped up, she tapped 'install' and quietly waited for it to finish. Then, she opened the app and looked at the login info again, entering it into the appropriate locations and hitting 'submit.'

And I'm in, she thought as the member landing page opened. Unfamiliar with the site, she got herself situated, figuring out where messages were, where her profile could be viewed, how to make changes and whatnot. After all, who knew what Carla had written about her after giving her a name like 'Dirty Hoe.' Her first step was to "hide" her profile since she wasn't interested in accumulating any more "likes" at this point. Then, she opened her own profile—as created by Carla—and sucked in a breath as she prepared to review the content.

Wow. Not bad, actually.

As it turned out, using the photos of Gia in the garden and removing the kids had been a brilliant idea. Not only did the profile fit perfectly with the *Only Gardeners* theme, but she had to admit she looked good, too! She noticed several areas where Carla may have overdone it a bit with the photo editing and filtering, but all in all, it worked—and none of it made her cringe. In truth, even the descriptive portions and 'What I'm Looking For' were pretty spot-on. Finding most of it acceptable, Gia made no changes. It was hidden now, anyway!

Moment of truth, Gia thought. *The messages.* She navigated to the right page on the site and saw it was jam-packed with greetings from a wide range of men. Some looked like actual farmers and gardeners, donning overalls, some more like lumberjacks in thick flannels, while others looked as far removed from a garden as they could possibly get—leather jackets and tight jeans. *I guess anyone can be into gardening.* Gia ignored them all, scrolling down with only one name on her mind—and there it was.

"... Ben," Gia said aloud, more breathily than she'd intended or anticipated. There, in the messages section, was one with Ben's profile image beside it. He looked good. Older, sure, but no less handsome. With one click, she would see the back-and-forth between him and Carla/Matt, which, as far as Ben was aware, was a discourse with Gia herself. Her hands felt frozen and heavy, but she managed to make them move to click open the series of messages.

As Carla had promised, there wasn't much to see. It was confirmed as no more than some initial pleasantries and the repeated suggestion by Ben to meet in person... and to discuss Aiden. Now, though, it was time to see where this would lead. Shaking, Gia began to draft a message. Her first *real* message to Ben since he'd left for Brazil after high school—since he'd left her alone and pregnant with his child. She couldn't find the words to say anything of much consequence, so she kept it simple.

Ben,
    We can meet if you want. Do you still drink coffee?
Gia

Gia glanced at the status circle that indicated whether Ben was online—he wasn't. With no telling when he would get on to read the message, Gia figured she'd better find something to do to keep busy, given that she had the whole day without her children. While weeds were a constant struggle out in the garden, she'd managed to pull a significant amount before Carla arrived, setting this new chaos into motion. She thought for a moment, then decided it was as good a day as any to harvest the basil for pesto, her favorite. After many smaller harvests that year, the plants had gotten somewhat out of control. What she loved most about basil —besides the flavor, of course—was that the more often she harvested it, the bigger and more robust the plants grew.

Being out in the garden earlier, Gia was already dressed for the task. She walked to the back door and pulled on a pair of waterproof gardening clogs. They weren't the sexiest footwear, but they were her favorite for days in the garden. She only planned on spending a short amount of time out there, and then she'd come in and prepare the pesto.

Gia walked across the yard to a small, fenced area with a wooden gate. She swung it open and walked into the herb garden. As she paced down a row between two raised garden beds, brushing against several plants, the intoxicating aromas of fresh herbs greeted her. Lavender and sage wafted through the air, triggering her to pluck a sage leaf and crush it between her fingers, closing her eyes for a moment as she raised it to her nostrils to inhale the scent. Herbs held a particular sort of magic to her. Not only were they delicious—each in their own way—but she found that their scents grounded her, giving her a deep sense of comfort and well-being, even during the most challenging days.

Gia was convinced of the healing power of herbal remedies, in addition to their food and aromatherapeutic benefits. Peppermint could not only refresh and invigorate the senses, triggering deeper focus, but it could also ease a stomachache. Its essential oil, which she'd long ago learned to make from her plants, could stop her headaches in their tracks when rubbed on the nape of the neck and temples. Crushed, dried lavender in a sachet or infused into a room and linen spray promoted high-quality sleep. She could go on and on about using herbs—to anyone who would listen—but for now, she needed basil for simple, delicious, organic, garden-fresh food!

Gia took one last whiff of the sage in her hand, popped the leaf into her mouth, and headed to the back of the fenced area where she had several basil plants. It didn't take long for her to harvest a whole basket full of the herbs, so she grabbed several bunches of chives, garlic chives, and scallions while she was out there. Each could be added to the pesto to up the flavor profile a notch. There was no recipe, and the tangy herbal mixture could be used as a dip, a spread, over pasta, or in various other ways.

Gia typically just tossed in what she thought would make it

work, and it came out delicious every time. The only thing to be mindful of was the ratio of liquid—in the form of high-quality olive oil—to solids to ensure the right texture. Usually, she added basil, a few other herbs, garlic she'd harvested previously, pine nuts or sunflower seeds, parmesan cheese, and whatever else struck her fancy! However, she'd made pesto using a variety of greens—from foraged mustard greens or nasturtium flower leaves to spinach or arugula.

Finally, Gia had what she needed. She gathered her herb-cutting shears, gardening gloves, and the basket laden with various herbs, mostly basil, and carried them out through the wooden gate. The cell phone in her back pocket buzzed as she reached the other side and closed it behind her. Out of habit, she pulled it out and checked the notifications...

"Ben," Gia spoke aloud, her breath catching in her chest. Glancing at the phone a second time, just to be sure, she confirmed it. At the top of the cell phone screen was an icon of a gardening hoe—the *Only Gardeners* app icon. She swiped up to see the complete notification and read to herself: *You have a new message from Ben.*

Gia took several steps away from the gate, landing in a seated position with her legs swung to the side of one of the lounge chairs she and Carla had spent many an afternoon on, laughing and drinking wine. She clicked open *Only Gardeners* and braced herself for... she didn't even know.

A Different Kind of Distraction

CARLA

As CARLA SQUEEZED through the missing post of the fence, returning from her morning visit to Gia to confess her sins, she thought, *Well, that could have gone worse.* She trotted across her own yard, climbed the deck steps, and entered her home through the sliding glass door.

Within moments, she saw Matt sitting on the couch, feet up on the ottoman, TV on. Carla could tell he was trying to act nonchalant, but she knew he'd been anxiously awaiting her return—and a recap of what transpired. She caught Matt's stare. "What?"

"Well?" Matt gazed at her quizzically.

"Well, what?"

"How did it go? I mean, you're back. You aren't in tears. I can only imagine it wasn't a total disaster... Right?"

Carla released a long-held sigh of relief and sat beside Matt on the couch. She wouldn't torture him any longer and filled him in on the events of her brief talk with Gia. "Surprisingly well, actually. She doesn't even seem that mad. It's almost like she knew something like this would happen eventually. Or that somehow people would find out."

"Well, there's no surprise there. I mean, you're Gia's best friend, and you're not exactly easy to keep secrets from! Even when they don't come out willingly," Matt teased. He quickly changed the subject when he saw Carla's shoulders hunch guiltily, moving the discussion away from Carla's inability to mind her own business and back to Gia. "So, what's she going to do?"

"Honestly, I don't know. I don't think *she* even knows yet. I think she needs to process it all. I gave her the login information for the *Only Gardeners* profile. She wants to see the conversations for herself."

"That makes sense," Matt said. "Do you think she's going to reach out to him?"

"I mean, I think she has to, right?" Matt rubbed his chin, seemingly deep in thought. "It's his kid—and there's no debating it. It only takes one good, solid look at the two of them to recognize that. Honestly, I don't know why none of us figured it out sooner." Carla raised her fingers to her mouth out of anxiety over the whole situation.

"Who would have guessed that Ben and Gia were ever even a thing, let alone that they slept together and had a child right out of high school?" Matt grabbed Carla's hand and pulled it away from her face. "Don't bite your nails. They're too pretty."

Carla blushed and allowed Matt to place her hand in his lap, holding it snuggly in his. "Yeah, I guess so." Carla shrugged. "Not knowing what she's going to say is killing me!"

"Well, all we can do is sit back and wait... I hope that, eventually, she fills us in on the details. And if not, Carla, for the love of God and all our sanity, please mind your own business. We BOTH mind our own business. No more meddling. Got it?"

"Yes, Matty, I promise. I think maybe I learned my lesson this time."

Matt let out a chuckle. "I highly doubt that," he said, rolling his eyes. "But, I guess time will tell!" Still holding Carla's hand in his lap, he wrapped his other arm around her waist and pulled her closer. "Now that this chaos has subsided, can we get back to our regularly scheduled programming?" Matt gave Carla an exaggerated wink and slid her hand over the bulge in his pants.

"Mmm," Carla purred. "What exactly did you have in mind?"

"I can think of several of our favorite activities I wouldn't mind revisiting," Matt flirted, kissing Carla softly behind the ear, then on the side of her neck.

"Matty, I'm sorry about all of this."

"Shhhh," Matt said. "No more talking." Matt released Carla's hand and slid one arm under her back and the other beneath her knees, lifting her with him in his arms as he rose from the couch. Carla wrapped both arms around his neck and rested her head against his chest, nuzzling him to take in his scent. He was her comfort. He was her home. He was everything she wanted for Gia and the very reason she'd gone behind her friend's back in the first place. *I've made so many mistakes in my life, but Gia is so good. If I have this, she deserves all of it and more,* Carla thought as Matt carried her upstairs to their bedroom as if she weighed no more than a child.

Still holding Carla in his arms, Matt leaned forward and pulled the blankets down using one hand before setting her down on the bed and situating the pillows so she could rest her head comfortably. He pushed a stray hair out of her face, tucking it gently behind her ear before placing his lips against hers. As their lips met, Carla couldn't help but wonder how their spark was still there after so many years—every time.

Carla couldn't get enough of Matt and knew he felt the same. She momentarily pulled away from Matt's lips and muttered, "Everyone should have this."

"Mmmhmm," Matt replied. "It's about to get better." Matt began kissing gentle, light kisses across the features of Carla's face, beginning on her forehead, then nose, then cheeks, before moving down. He kissed the side of her neck, lingering for a moment, nibbling her ear lobe gently, then doing the same on the other side.

Carla felt dizzy. Good dizzy. Matt always made her feel that way. He continued toward Carla's chest, taking a moment to raise her arms above her head and carefully lift her shirt over her head before unclasping her bra and removing it. His lips moved to her breast, taking a nipple gently between his teeth as his other hand wandered to the opposite side, gently cupping, pinching, and caressing.

"Matt, don't stop," Carla urged.

"My love, I have absolutely no intention of stopping anytime soon. We can be at this all day if you want. Now, close your eyes and relax. I want to taste you."

"Mmm, I love you."

"I love you, too."

Matt lingered at Carla's chest for a few more moments, teasing her with his fingers and mouth before running his fingers down to her stomach and the top of her abdomen. His hands moved gently under the waist of her pants, pulling them downward and then tossing them to the floor, leaving Carla lying before him in only her panties. He took in the sight before him, admiring her striking beauty and well-toned body. "You're so beautiful, my princess," he muttered.

Carla let out a moan. She had a thing for pet names—and 'princess' really got her going, a fact Matt was well aware of. She raised her hips, silently urging Matt to continue. He took the hint, sliding her panties down her legs and bringing his lips to one side of her hips with a gentle kiss, then the other. His mouth moved to her lower abdomen, slowly placing another kiss just below her belly button.

Matt placed a hand against Carla's inner thigh and pushed hard, spreading her legs wide. His kisses slowly made their way to her pussy, tongue teasing around her lips and the edges of her folds, circling her clit slowly and sensually. Matt continued to lick, suck, and tease Carla, his tongue diving inside as her hips rose to meet his mouth. Matt could tell she was close to an orgasm when she reached her arms forward and held his head, pressing him deeper into her. Carla's hips rose and fell to meet Matt's mouth as he licked with more pressure against her clit in response to her fingers intertwined in his hair.

"Oh my God, Matt. Matt, don't sto—" Carla hadn't even finished her sentence when her climax hit. She dug her fingernails into him as her entire body clenched and tightened, blissful sensations coming in waves, leaving her spent but fulfilled. Matt pulled away from Carla, wiping his face with his hand before collapsing next to her on the bed, allowing her to wrap her body around his, intertwining their limbs.

"Feel better?" Matt asked.

"Mmhmm," Carla responded, shaky and unable to find any actual words yet.

"Good. Rest up for a bit. There's more where that came from. I have a few other ideas to keep us occupied until we hear from Gia." Matt grinned and pulled Carla close, knowing their afternoon was just getting started.

"I love you, Matty."

"Love you, too, princess."

"Your turn next," Carla promised.

Arrangements

GIA

Chapter 19

Her hands trembling slightly, Gia navigated the *Only Gardeners* app, arriving in the messages folder and seeing the unopened envelope icon next to Ben's profile image. She breathed deep into her lungs and held it for several seconds before releasing it and clicking the message open.

> *Dear Gia,*
>
> *Do you know me? How could I ever give up coffee? Especially after living in Brazil—some of the best in the world there. Just say where and when...*
>
> *Ben*

Gia rolled her eyes. She knew he didn't say it to be intention-ally insensitive, but the mention of Brazil rubbed her the wrong way. After all, she had given up the potentially life-changing expe-rience Brazil offered for an entirely different life by choosing Aiden. She chose her child. And, while she had absolutely no regrets about that decision, the mention of Brazil and how Ben had chosen that adventure over her and Aiden still stung. It was as if Ben had pulled the scab off a still-healing wound with a single message.

Gia began typing.

Ben,
   I wouldn't kno—

Realizing she was about to respond very passive-aggressively, Gia deleted the start of her message and began again.

Ben,
   I'm sure they have excellent coffee. The café on Main Street has decent drinks—maybe not Brazilian, but not bad. I can meet you there tomorrow after my kids get off to school. We can talk then, but I can't stay long.
   Gia

Gia needed to keep things short and sweet. She didn't want to get caught up in anything emotional. This was strictly business. She would keep all of their discussion about Aiden. She knew they would have to meet eventually and that there would likely be some tough conversations ahead between her, her ex-husband, Aiden, and Ben... but for the time being, to maintain her sanity until the next day, emotions had to stay out of it. She was already overwhelmed with nostalgia and some bitterness from remem-bering their past the night before.

The little green circle over Ben's image told her that he was currently online, and it took only moments for her message to change from 'sent' to 'read,' indicating that Ben had probably been awaiting her response. *His turn,* Gia thought. Despite her best efforts to avoid seeming overanxious, she couldn't help herself. She placed her hand on her knee to stop her leg from bouncing, a dead giveaway indicating her nerves were on edge as she awaited another message from Ben. Luckily, she was alone.

It didn't take long for her phone to vibrate again, with the new message icon appearing again at the top of the screen. She steadied her hands and read:

Gia,

Is 9 AM tomorrow okay?

This time, Ben didn't sign his name formally at the bottom of the message, which Gia took to indicate it was becoming more of a back-and-forth chat than individual messages. She pulled open the calendar app on her phone to double-check her schedule tomorrow—something she realized should have been done before telling him she was available the next day in the first place. *Perfect. I'm free until around 10, then a doctor's appointment in the same area of town.*

Gia smiled to herself. A ten o'clock doctor's appointment meant she could easily escape the meeting without concocting an excuse. She was a terrible liar and tried avoiding it whenever possible because people always knew. Even her 'little white lies' were blatantly obvious! Gia left the formal greeting off her message to acknowledge their ongoing discussion.

Gia: Nine is good. I have a doctor's appointment, so I can't stay long.

Ben: You said that already.

Gia: Just reiterating.

Ben: Okay, then. See you at nine tomorrow at the Café on Main—Cold Brew, right? Good coffee.

Gia: See you at nine.

Gia recognized she was being blunt but refused to allow herself to get emotionally tied up in this before even seeing Ben. Maybe there would be more emotion during their meeting, or perhaps she could manage to keep it all business. Either way, this wasn't the time for getting all swept up in the past. She had to maintain her composure. Her children would be back from her ex-husband's house soon, and Gia wanted to keep this from them for as long as she could—at least until she and Ben sorted out what it all meant. *What does he want from all this? Why is he back?*

She couldn't help but wonder what role Ben hoped to play in Aiden's—and her—lives. As Aiden's father, she wouldn't begrudge his meeting with his son, but at the same time, he had abandoned them both. Coming back now, especially after Aiden had grown up knowing an entirely different father figure, would only complicate things.

What is he really entitled to beyond meeting Aiden? Gia scoffed to herself. She couldn't help but let a hint of anger tinge her thoughts. It wasn't fair for Ben to think he could simply swoop back in and shake up her son's entire world, not to mention her's. He had a choice many years ago, and he made it. It didn't include them, so why should it now? *We owe him nothing,* Gia thought. *Nothing at all. If he wants into our lives in any capacity, he's got a lot of making it up to us to do.*

Even so, Gia couldn't help but let her mind—and heart—wander in the direction of some sort of romantic reunion. Was that what he wanted? Or was this solely about Aiden? After all, he was on a dating site—and so was she. Gia gave a gentle slap to her own face, scolding herself. *No, Gia. Never again. Don't even think it.*

Gia rose from where she remained perched on the edge of the lounge chair, grabbed her garden harvest, and wandered into the house, heading toward the kitchen. She needed to return to her earlier distraction and get her mind off things. "Pesto time," she said aloud, pulling the carefully bunched basil and herbs out of her basket and giving them a quick rinse under running water. Once she started moving around the kitchen, Gia knew she was a force to be reckoned with. Depending on her mood, she could whip up a mouthwatering cold dish in mere minutes or spend hours crafting and cooking the perfect comfort food.

Gia firmly believed that the best food always came from the freshest ingredients—and as far as she was concerned, nothing topped the produce from her garden. It made her feel good that she was significantly more self-sustainable—and ecologically friendly—than most of her friends when it came to feeding her family.

Gia pulled out the food processor, tossing in garlic and parmesan cheese as she tried to force her mind off the current situation playing out in her life. Lately, it almost felt like it wasn't her own. Everything had been so dramatic over the past year, and it felt like she was on the outside looking in, jaw dropped low in shock as the hits just kept coming. She needed some sort of reprieve, some sort of... something!

As her mind wandered, she added the remaining ingredients to the food processor. She turned it on, pushing the pulse button repeatedly, allowing the machine to combine the ingredients until the mixture had reached the desired consistency. As she worked, she couldn't help but think about how this was one of Carla and Matt's favorites. Maybe she would bring them some as a peace offering to show them she wasn't mad—not *that* mad, anyway.

She *was* in a way, but Gia knew she couldn't stay angry with Carla for very long. It simply wasn't possible. Despite everything, Carla was always there for her, especially over the past year. Gia also knew it would be driving her friend crazy that she was still in the dark over precisely what had happened between her and Ben originally—and where things stood now that Gia had the *Only Gardeners* login info.

She dialed Carla's cell phone number. It rang several times more than she had expected under the circumstances. She was just about to hang up when Carla finally picked up.

Farewell

CARLA

"CARLA?" Matt said sleepily, receiving no response. "Carla, your phone is ringing," he repeated, giving his wife a gentle prod in the ribs. Carla rolled over sleepily.

"Huh?" Carla glanced at her vibrating phone. "I'll get it later. I sleepy sleep." They'd spent the past couple of hours in bed, contented with using each other as their distraction from the Gia and Ben situation. At some point, they must have fallen back to sleep. Matt grabbed the buzzing phone, prepared to hit 'ignore' on the call to send it to voicemail.

Matt glanced at the name on the lit-up screen of Carla's phone. "You sure? It's Gia."

Carla shot up in the bed, grabbing the phone from Matt's

hand and throwing it against her ear as she hit the green 'answer' button.

"Hello? Gia? What's up? What's going on? Everything good? Are you good?" The words rushed from Carla's mouth in a rapid-fire, jumbled mess.

"Whoa, slow down. Everything is fine," Gia started. "I made pesto!"

"You—you made pesto? That's all you have to tell me right now? *You made pesto?*" Carla's face morphed into a frown, and she couldn't hold the question in for another second. "What happened with Ben?!"

Gia chuckled, surprised Carla had held it in even that long. She'd expected "What happened with Ben?" to be the very first words out of her friend's mouth when she answered the phone.

"Well, you're making progress. It took a full 27 seconds for that question to escape," Gia pointed out. "Listen, I'll tell you everything. Can I come over? I'll bring pesto!"

"As if you need to bribe me to come over and fill in the blanks. Yes! Come over!" Carla glanced down, and, realizing she and Matt were both still naked, she added, "Uh, give me—us— fifteen minutes, though."

"Okay, back patio. Fifteen minutes." Gia hung up the phone, grabbing the loaf of Italian bread from the bread box. She tossed it into the oven without preheating it first, just to warm it up. Pesto could be used in many ways, but Gia knew Carla and Matt loved it spread on bread.

Carla rolled over and kicked her legs over the side of the bed. "Matty, Gia is coming over. She's bringing food."

"Ooh, I love when she brings food!" Matt laughed, sliding behind Gia on the bed and wrapping his legs around Carla's waist as she tried to rise. "But does she have to come *right* now?" Matt put his arms around her neck gently from behind.

"Come on, Matty. We've been in here all morning. It's time to get moving! If you don't let me go, we'll both wind up greeting Gia naked," she said, chuckling.

"Threesome?" Matt suggested, a teasing grin forming on his lips. Carla feigned being offended.

"Never. You're mine. All mine. You're stuck with me."

"And, Carla, my love, you're all the woman I can handle!" Matt released the grip his arms and legs held around Carla, allowing her to get up. She turned her head, gave him a quick peck on the lips, and walked over to her dresser, pulling out a clean pair of jeans and a T-shirt.

"Yeah, yeah, yeah. Get dressed!"

"Yes, ma'am," Matt said, getting up and grabbing his own clothes. They both dressed and made their way downstairs and toward the kitchen. Matt poured two tall glasses of water, added a quick squeeze of lemon to each, and pulled open the door to the back patio. Gia wasn't there yet, but they sat at the table to await her arrival, setting their drinks down on the same tabletop where the game of *Twenty Questions* had triggered Gia's rapid departure the last time.

A few minutes later, Gia appeared at the fence, sliding through the small opening and walking across the yard carrying a foil-wrapped loaf of bread and a bowl of what they could only assume was pesto. She sat down in an empty chair and began unwrapping the foil, revealing a pre-cut loaf of bread, still warm.

"Didn't bring a knife," Gia said. "We're dipping."

As Gia pried the lid off the bowl, Matt and Carla wasted no time. They each grabbed a slice of bread and dipped it into the pesto—more like a scoop than a dip, really.

"Mmmm, the bread is warm," Carla said to no one in particular, returning her bread to the bowl for a double dip.

"Hurry up! You're hogging the pesto!" Matt scolded, a smile dancing behind his fake scowl.

Carla rolled her eyes. "Okay, okay. Have some. Anyway, we have things to discuss. Right, Gia?"

Gia chuckled. "I suppose we do. I don't even know where to start, honestly."

"The beginning is usually good," Carla said. Matt could only add a nod, his mouth full with a large bite of bread and dip.

Gia sighed, her hands clenched together, trying to keep from fidgeting. "Alright... the beginning. It started the summer after graduation. The summer that you spent traveling. Ben and I became close after we met at the World Corps presentation. I was signed up to go to Brazil, too."

"But you never lived in Brazil," Carla rubbed her chin thoughtfully.

"No. I didn't. I had Aiden instead."

"What were you and Ben like... to each other? Were you dating?"

"It's complicated. I don't even know what we were. We had plans to travel together and be together in some capacity during World Corps. I think we were both kind of waiting until we went to Brazil to figure it all out. Then—well, that didn't happen."

"Did he know you were pregnant when he left?"

"He knew."

Gia

Gia took a deep breath, remembering the moment she learned that Ben would still be going to Brazil despite knowing she was pregnant with Aiden. It was the last time she saw or heard from him. He had made his decision, and it didn't involve her or their baby—so Aiden became *her* baby.

"Gia, I can't have a kid right now. We are too young. You're too young. This changes everything. Everything we talked about, all we were going to do—our lives. World Corps. Everything!" Ben said.

"Do you think I don't know that?" Gia's face reddened; she was perfectly aware of what this turn of events meant for her life plans. Her heart beat faster in her chest in a combination of anger and fear over what was to come.

"Gia, we can fix this. You don't have to have this baby. Or, you can have it and give it up for adoption, then meet me down in Brazil."

"You're still planning to go—even without me? Even knowing about the baby?"

"Gia, this has always been my plan. I can't just give this up. It's my only ticket out of this town. You can still come—or you can meet me next year." Ben's hands shook as he spoke.

"Meet you with a baby I've taken care of alone for a year? How can you be so insensitive?" Gia asked, burying her face in her hands and trying to hold back the sobs threatening to escape. Her chest began to rise and fall faster, heaving as the tears welled up in her eyes.

"Gia, I'm not trying to be insensitive. I'm really not. I just... I just don't know what to do here." Ben's shoulders were hunched over, and he looked defeated but committed to his decision. "We are too young," Ben said. "We are just too young..." His voice trailed off as he gazed at Gia, and the sobs began to emerge.

"Obviously not too young to get pregnant, though!" spat Gia, now angry. She felt abandoned and alone during what she could only guess would be one of the most challenging times of her life. "Get out!" she roared, causing Ben to step backward toward the door out of surprise. "Get out now! I never want to see you again!"

"Gia, I—"

"Leave!" Gia folded her arms across her chest, tears streaming, as Ben stood uncomfortably, now at the entry to her room.

"I'm sorry. I'm so, so sorry," Ben said as he turned and walked down the stairs. And that was it. That was the last time Gia saw or heard from him—and a turning point in her life.

❧

From that moment on, Gia considered the baby growing inside her as hers alone until a few months later when she met her now ex-husband, Steve. Steve was everything Ben wasn't at the time—older, more financially stable, and absolutely enamored by Gia from their first introduction. They had met at a fundraising event for the local garden project. Steve was a local real estate agent and wanted to "give back to the community" through the project, having done well for himself through several lucrative property deals the year prior. He wasn't particularly into gardening, but it seemed to him as good a cause as any!

Gia and Steve hit it off immediately—first as friends. However, as he helped her and acted as a source of support throughout the pregnancy, a more intimate relationship blossomed. She leaned heavily on him, and while she never felt the same sparks as she had with Ben, it seemed safer that way. Still, somehow, she always felt like she was playing a role with Steve—merely acting out the motions of the good wife and mother, but never truly herself. In a way, it was as if she was hiding the fact that she felt more like a child he had signed up to care for. She tried to keep her vulnerability and abandonment issues a secret and they gnawed at her.

Steve proposed quickly, knowing Aiden was well on his way, and Gia accepted, thinking it the most responsible option. He was looking for a family and took Aiden in as if he were his own from birth. In all honesty, it was primarily the reason Gia married the man. Sure, she loved him back then, but it wasn't the type of love that would—or should—have led to marriage had it not been for Aiden and the stability Steve offered.

I guess that's why we're divorced now, Gia thought and chuckled.

The Pesto Party

CARLA

Chapter 21

"HE KNEW ABOUT AIDEN, and he left anyway?" Carla asked, the concern in her voice snapping Gia back to reality.

"Yep."

"I'm so sorry, Gia. I wish I'd been here to help. If I'd known, I would have figured out a way to be there for you."

"Carla, you were off doing your own thing. We were young! By the time you came back, I'd already met Steve. And he was great back then. We hit it off immediately, and things just fell into place. He took Aiden in as if he were his own biological child. We were fine."

"So, you married Steve... but you loved Ben?"

"It was complicated. Steve and I rushed things, knowing

Aiden was well on his way—but I wouldn't give it all up for anything, even with how things worked out with my marriage. Ben's choice led me to Steve, which gave me my other children. They're my world."

"What about seeing Ben now? Do you think there's anything left to explore there?" Carla peered quizzically at Gia, wondering whether she held onto any lingering emotional attachment. The look that flashed through her eyes indicated something was there, but Gia quickly brushed her feelings aside, her features becoming stony once more.

"After the pain Ben caused, I'll never feel that way—or any way at all—about him ever again," Gia said, folding her arms across her chest. "Even after I met Steve, healing from that took a long time. I'm *still* processing everything, many years later. A lot of it resurfaced when Steve left, honestly. It's a consistent nagging feeling that I'll never be enough for anyone."

"You're enough for me. And Matt loves you, too, right Matty?"

Matt was caught off-guard by the question and had a mouthful of the bread and pesto he was devouring, so he nodded his agreement while chewing.

"Matt!" Carla prodded him in the ribs with her elbow. "That's for *everyone*. It's not Matt's personal pesto platter." She rolled her eyes at her husband, grabbed a piece of bread, and dipped it into the bowl, hurrying to get her share before the rest disappeared.

"Oof, sorry." Matt chuckled, wiping away the green herbal concoction that had escaped his mouth and was now running down his chin. "It's just so good. So, so good."

"And, in case you were wondering," Carla reverted to her original train of thought, "that's man talk. Translated, it means he loves you... and your garden... and your always-incredible food contributions."

"Well, thanks," Gia said, smiling.

"Who needs a Steve or a Ben when you have a Carla and a

Matt right next door, anyway?!" Carla patted her friend on the shoulder playfully, hoping her mood was improving.

Gia

Gia grinned at her friend. Despite Carla's inability to mind her own business, she could cheer Gia up even under the worst circumstances. *And your child's biological father returning from an entirely different life in a foreign country when your child doesn't even know he exists is pretty bad.*

"Anyway, I'm meeting him tomorrow morning at the café on Main," Gia said, fidgeting nervously.

With a mouth full of bread, Carla appeared stunned and chewed faster to get her words out. "That's fast! Are you going to let him meet his son? How are you going to tell Aiden? What about Steve?" The questions came out in rapid fire. Gia had to brace herself to respond as calmly as possible.

"Yes, I can't keep him from Aiden. I mean, I could. Ben abandoned us—but I don't think it would be right to stand in the way if he wants to meet him. I haven't figured out what to tell my son. That's a conversation I'll need to have with Steve before anything else. Steve has always been Aiden's father and remains so. I want to talk to Ben first to determine his true intentions with all of this. And... that's happening tomorrow!" Gia took a deep breath as the rush of emotions built back up.

"Do you want me to go with you?" Carla asked. "Like, for moral support or something? Matt could come, too, in case you need someone to kick his ass." She grinned, trying to lighten the mood. Matt folded his arms across his chest and firmed up his features, trying to look more intimidating.

"No, I'm okay. This needs to be a one-on-one meeting. I have a doctor's app—"

"We could sit on the other side of the café. We can be stealthy!"

"Carla, don't start this again!" Matt nudged his wife. "We've been through this. You've done enough. We've done enough."

"Thanks, Matt. Carla, promise me that you won't show up. Please." Gia glanced at her friends as she made the request, feeling calmer knowing they had her back—even if she didn't want their physical presence at the café the next day. *Now,* she thought, *if they could just learn to mind their own business.*

"What if I need coffee?" Carla asked. "I love coffee. I love café coffee!"

"First off, you don't leave the house by nine *ever.* If you feel compelled to do so tomorrow, you wait. Until ten. Before nine or after ten, the café is *all* yours. Just don't appear during that one-hour window."

"Why ten? What happens at ten?"

"I was trying to say this earlier. At ten, I bail for my doctor's appointment, regardless of how things are going. Ben gets one hour, tops."

"Ooh, that's convenient," Carla said. "What do you think he wants with Aiden? Like, does he just want to meet him as a friend of yours? Does he want him to know everything about who he is? How much does he want to be involved?"

"You're asking the same things floating around in my mind. I have absolutely no idea. I won't know anything until after tomorrow. I'll fill you in, I promise." A teasing smirk crossed Gia's features. "Especially given that this is all your fault."

"Ugh. I know, I know. You don't have to rub it in. And anyway, Ben would have found you eventually. And, hey, maybe your—well, my—chance meeting on *Only Gardeners* was the hand of fate pushing you two crazy kids back together!"

Gia groaned. "Trust me. It wasn't. It was merely a friend who couldn't keep out of trouble. And, for the record, we are *not* getting back together."

Carla leaned over and placed her hands jokingly over Matt's

ears and fake whispered, "But he got really fucking cute, though! Wait until you see him to decide."

"I can still *hear* you, you know?" Matt said, removing Carla's hands and wrapping them around his neck in an embrace. "But the guy is attractive. From a heterosexual male perspective, anyway."

"I saw his pictures," Gia acknowledged. "I admit, he's good-looking. He certainly grew up while he was in Brazil, that's for sure. But I'm not interested. I'll never be interested."

"What's that they say about famous last words?" Carla chuckled.

Emotion Sickness

~∽~

GIA

Chapter 22

THE NEXT MORNING, Gia stood before her open closet, a growing pile of discarded clothes on the floor beside her. She had set her alarm early to give her extra time to get ready in case she had any jitters about seeing Ben for the first time in what felt like a lifetime. *Why do I care what I am wearing? I don't care! This is about Aiden's father. That's it.* Gia kept telling herself the same thing: She didn't care. But, still, she couldn't help but feel she needed to look her best—but also like she wasn't trying too hard.

She wanted Ben to regret leaving, to see what he had missed out on by choosing Brazil over her and Aiden and having a life together. She wouldn't admit it, even to herself, but she wanted him to have regrets. Finally, after an eternity of picking apart her wardrobe, Gia's eyes fell on an old shirt, a very old shirt—one that she hadn't worn in what felt like... a lifetime. It was one of Ben's favorites from "way back then," and for whatever reason, through shifting sizes and pregnancies and countless closet revamps, she hadn't been able to throw it away or donate it.

It was fairly simple, an off-one-shoulder top that hadn't ever really gone into *or* out of style—except maybe during the 80s—but that Gia had always felt highlighted her best features. It certainly didn't give off the appearance of 'trying too hard,' and she wondered if Ben would remember it. Doubtful, but still an interesting experiment nonetheless.

Gia threw on a pair of skinny jeans and a long tank top, then pulled the other shirt over her head, tugging it downward until it hugged her hips. "A little tighter than I remember, but... it works," Gia said aloud with a shrug as she gazed at her reflection in the mirror. *Not bad,* she thought. A glance at the clock told her it was time to start making moves. Ben would be at the coffee shop in just about an hour, and she wanted to give herself plenty of time to get there and park downtown as it was often busy at that time of day.

"Alright, let's do this." She gave herself a final check in the mirror before walking down the stairs, grabbing her purse and keys, and heading out the door. Fortunately, the drive was an easy one, so she was able to put on some music and work on her breathing in an attempt to remove any expectations about the meeting. Gia had decided it was better to go into it with an open mind.

By the time she pulled into a parking space in the municipal lot near the coffee shop, her mind was spinning despite her best efforts to remain calm, cool, and collected. She couldn't help but wonder where this was all leading, what she would tell Aiden, how her ex-husband would react, and whether seeing Ben again after so many years would be awkward. "Breathe, Gia. Just breathe. Everything will be fine. It's only Ben," she told herself.

Only Ben? Ben had changed her life in ways that couldn't be undone.

Gia shook her head a few times, a physical manifestation of shaking it off. A glance at the clock in the center of her car dashboard told her it was about time to head over to the café. She wanted to arrive first to get a coffee and find a table, thereby avoiding any awkward '*Who's paying?*' moments, although Gia couldn't help but acknowledge Ben owed her a whole lot more than a cup of coffee after leaving her alone to raise his child.

She stepped out of her car, popped a few quarters into the parking meter, and headed toward the café on Main. As she stepped under the sign reading *Cold Brew: The Café on Main,* Gia remembered when the coffee shop was known strictly as *The Café on Main.* New owners had come in, re-branded, and added the rest of the name but kept the original as a nod to loyal, long-time customers. Gia hadn't returned to the shop much since the switch, as her coffee budget had dropped dramatically. Her children's food, clothes, and activities had gotten more expensive over time as they grew into new interests—even with help from her ex-husband, they were far from well-off, and every dime was accounted for.

As Gia stepped inside, she inhaled deeply. The aroma of freshly brewed coffee filled the air, a treat for her senses. *Cold Brew* was cozy and comfortable, with soft lighting and an entire room back room filled with plush seating areas surrounding a central fireplace. The front featured the coffee bar and bakery cases, offering tables and chairs that catered to those sitting to drink their coffee and have a quick bite. The back had become a haven for remote workers, book readers, writers, and those seeking a longer respite from their busy day-to-day lives. The walls featured art from local artists as well as those from communities around the globe where the coffee was sourced, adding to the eclectic ambiance.

Gia walked up to the counter. She was about to place a coffee order when she heard her name.

"Gia! Over here. I have your coffee and cruller," a familiar voice called. It felt like a shock to the system to hear Ben's voice saying her name—now older, more adult. They weren't young kids when he'd left. Still, as she turned her head to face Ben, she couldn't help but notice how much he'd grown up and filled out... in a good way. She imagined she had changed as well. Quite frankly, she imagined she looked worn out.

Gia walked over to the two-seater table where Ben sat, a slight smile formed across her lips as she glanced down and saw the cruller on the plate in front of the empty seat. *He remembered—the French cruller: my go-to sweet breakfast treat.* Ben jumped up to pull Gia's chair out, ushering her to sit. Gia couldn't decide whether she was offended that Ben thought he still knew her well enough to order for her. *I'll be the judge of that,* she thought as she sipped the coffee before her. *Damn. Perfect.*

"Gia, you haven't changed a bit." Ben fidgeted nervously as he sat on the opposite side of the table.

"I find that hard to believe," Gia began. "It's been a long time. You've changed quite a bit." Gia raised her eyes to meet his but quickly lowered them as an unexpected emotional reaction tugged at her. *Don't cry, Gia. Don't cry.*

"Gia, it's been too long. I'm sorry." Ben reached across the table and placed his hand under Gia's chin, raising it so their eyes met again. "I've had a long time to think, and I'd be lying if I said I didn't have regrets. We were so young when... when everything happened. I didn't know anything about life or anything, really. I had a one-track mind and a single dream."

Gia didn't know how to respond or what to say. She searched her mind and could find no words, but tears began to well at the corners of her eyes.

"Don't cry, Gia. I'm sorry."

Then, the words finally came. They came ferociously and wouldn't stop flowing. Gia had so much to say—years of built-up anger, sadness, and hate, paired with a strange longing for what could have been but wasn't. Competing. It had become love versus hate, and the hate started pouring out at that moment.

"No," Gia started. "No, stop. You don't get to say 'sorry' and have it all just go away. You left me. You abandoned us. You moved forward while we were left behind without even a little bit of help. You didn't even check in on us to see how things were going. You didn't even call or wr—"

"I did, Gia. I did. I promise. You just didn't know it. I came back several times and always checked in secretly. I asked around. I didn't think trying to come back into your life was fair. You seemed happy with your—with your new husband and the baby. But I made sure you were okay. You got together with him really fast..."

"Not as fast as you walked out the door when we needed you most. I needed a father for *your* baby. I needed help! He was there for me. He was there for all of us. You, on the other hand, were not. You were off playing adventurer in the fucking Amazon rainforest without me."

"I know. I said I was sorry, but don't for a minute believe I didn't think about you and our son every single day I was gone."

"He's not your son. Only biologically. You don't even know him. You don't have the right to call him your son. You gave that up."

"I know. I want to know him, though, Gia. Let me get to know Aiden. Please? I'll do everything I can to make it up to you."

Suddenly, anger surged through Gia's body, overtaking her ability to remain calm. She shoved her chair away from the table, the ear-piercing sound of the its legs scraping against the floor causing other café patrons to wince as they turned to stare at the scene unfolding before them. Her face flushed and felt hot as she looked around and noticed so many eyes glued to her, but she brushed it off and rose to her feet, her eyes narrow.

"No. You won't—because you can't. It's not possible."

Gia rose and pushed her chair under the table in a swift

motion, then stormed toward the door, trying desperately to keep the tears from flowing until she reached her car.

"Gia! Wait!" Ben called after her. "Please, wait?" But she ignored his calls, which faded into the background noise as she got further away from the café. She wouldn't do this. She couldn't. Gia knew she needed to get away from Ben as quickly as possible.

Things certainly hadn't gone as planned. She hadn't expected to lose her composure or go off on him, but the emotions came tumbling down, and the words poured out like a torrent of water from a broken faucet. She had no power over the anger and rage she felt about the situation he'd left her and Aiden in so many years ago. When she finally opened her car door and collapsed inside, she buried her face in her hands and sobbed, finally letting years worth of tears escape the confines of the walls she'd built up to keep them in.

Mystery Woman

BEN

Chapter 23

"I DESERVED THAT," Ben said aloud to the many café customers still staring at him. Some chuckled, others gave him sympathetic looks, but slowly, the patrons lost interest in Ben as they realized the drama had already unfolded. Seeing the show was over, they returned to their laptops, books, pastries, and caffeine fixes, leaving Ben alone with his thoughts.

Shit. I messed up. Like, really messed up, Ben thought as he sat alone at the table for two in *Cold Brew.* The meeting hadn't gone as he'd hoped. He had spent so many years missing Gia, wishing things had been different, but it all imploded when he finally had a chance to make things right.

She hates me, he thought. *Totally hates me. I'm scum to her—*

and rightfully so. He had envisioned some sort of magical re-kindling of what they'd had before, an instant love connection in which the past was at least forgiven, if not forgotten.

I guess I'm going to have to work for this, thought Ben as he tilted his coffee cup back to finish the final gulp. He stood and walked out of the coffee shop, surprised to see a familiar figure walking down the street about a block away. It was Gia. She hadn't left the area yet. *That's right. She said she had an appointment nearby. Maybe if I try again?*

"Gia!" shouted Ben, trying to get her attention. Gia glanced over her shoulder, saw Ben, and began to walk faster—practically breaking into a jog. "Gia, please wait?" Ben begged as he ran to catch up. "I'm sorry about before. Can we talk?"

"I have a doctor's appointment," Gia said, gesturing to the building across the street. "I can't."

Ben looked into Gia's eyes. It was clear she'd been crying. They were hypnotizingly beautiful, but also puffy and red, and she still sniffled faintly, even though she tried to hide it. Ben took a chance without thinking or giving her a chance to recoil. He reached around Gia and pulled her close, holding her tightly in his arms. Just an embrace.

It worked.

Gia melted into him, exhausted from the emotional toll of the morning. Her head rested against his chest, and he could feel her body heave in and out, breathing in his scent. He wondered if she remembered the feeling of being held in his arms.

"Gia, I'm sorry. I promise. I'll make it up to you and Aiden," he whispered in her ear, triggering an entirely different response. Gia lifted her head abruptly, shoved Ben away, and bolted across the street and up the stairs toward the large, gray medical building that towered over them. Within moments, she was gone.

Ben raised his head toward the sky and rolled his eyes. "That could have gone better... again." He stood there for several minutes, hoping Gia would realize she'd made a mistake, turn around, and return to his embrace. He could have waited longer, hoping to catch her after her appointment, but that felt too stalk-erish. Ben walked toward his car and made his way home.

Upon arriving in his small apartment, he sat on the living room sofa, trying to process everything that had just happened. Burying his head in his hands, he rolled his neck back and forth a few times as he pondered his next steps. He had just grabbed his cell phone from his pocket to browse social media aimlessly to forget his circumstances when the *Only Gardeners* app caught his eye. *I wonder if she would answer...*

He began to type:

Dear Gia,

I'm sorry for how things worked out today. I'd like to talk to you again. I want to get everything between us out in the open, the good and the bad. I want to meet Aiden, and I don't think that can happen until you and I can be in the same room together without yelling or cryi—

No, she'll feel called out. She was the only one yelling or crying, thought Ben. He backspaced the last sentence and tried again:

I want to meet Aiden, but you and I have some things to iron out first. Maybe we should try someplace a little more private next time. No free show for the other Cold Brew patrons!

Ben

He considered removing the 'no free show' line but thought it was kind of funny, so he left it and hit the send button, putting the message out into the online dating world and hoping for the best. Just as he was about to close the app, Ben received a notif-ication. "You have one new like!"

Might as well take a look. He clicked the notification icon. The screen transitioned to an undeniably beautiful woman's profile. Her long black hair fell pin-straight down her back, and hazel eyes, brown specked with hints of green, gazed sexily out at him from within the screen. *She doesn't look like she's ever set foot in a garden, but I suppose looks can be deceiving.*

As Ben perused her profile, he received another notification —a new message.

> *Hey there. You're cute. Wanna hear a secret?*
> *Jen*

Ben rubbed his chin thoughtfully for a moment. Given how the morning with Gia had gone, he figured he might as well at least try to keep his options open. It's not like they were together. Or ever going to be. He began crafting his response.

> *Hey, Jen. I'm Ben. Jen and Ben, hey, that rhymes... Wow, I sound lame. I'd love to hear a secret if you're still reading after that.*
> *Ben*

> *My secret... is... that I don't actually have a garden. But I think men who garden are sexy. And I think **you're** sexy.*
> *Jen*

Having just sipped from his water bottle, Ben began coughing, causing water to drip down his chin. *Well, that was blunt.* It did, however, pique his interest.

> *Well, Jen, I'm having a bit of a rough day. Would you like to meet so I can treat you to lunch later today? I'd love the company of a beautiful woman—no expectations, just lunch.*
> *Ben*

> *I'd love that, but why wait? Are you free now? I'm finishing up an appointment downtown. We could grab something at one of the restaurants on Main Street.*

The two continued to communicate back and forth for several more minutes until they'd finalized their arrangements to meet downtown in just over an hour. Ben felt a little silly going back to the same area he'd just been for breakfast. Still, at the same time, he thought he needed company. And why not meet up with a beautiful woman? It wasn't like anyone else was jumping to date him—although he hadn't really been trying. The one woman he'd shown interest in before Jen messaged had just told him off and disappeared—twice.

Ben walked up to his room and began to freshen up. He didn't need very much prep time as he had already showered, dressed, and spritzed cologne earlier that morning in hopes of making a good impression on Gia. *Guess it takes more than expensive cologne,* Ben thought with a sigh. He finished getting ready, returned to his car, and headed off on his lunch date.

The plan was to meet at *Charmed to Table,* a newer farm-to-table restaurant in town. They'd have lunch, get to know one another, and see where things went. Both Jen and Ben had promised no expectations, only lunch! Despite the morning Ben had dealt with, he was looking forward to meeting someone new, even if it was primarily a much-needed distraction from everything else happening with Gia and Aiden.

Charmed to Table

CARLA

"HELLO?" Carla spoke into her phone, which had been ringing for several moments before she could find it. "Gia! What's up? How'd it go? No, not the doctor's visit! Ben! How'd it go with Ben?" Carla rolled her eyes. *Why would she be telling me about a routine visit to the doctor? For such a smart cookie, sometimes Gia can be a little dense. Then again, it's more likely she's probably trying to avoid the topic of Ben.*

"What? Oh, that doesn't sound good," Carla continued. "Slow down, slow down. Okay, yeah. I'll be there in a few minutes. Bring the gift card, though—lunch out isn't in my budget today!"

Carla rose to her feet in record time, leaving Matt staring at her in confusion, having only heard one side of the conversation. "Uh, Carla... Where ya going?"

"Oh, sorry! *Charmed to Table.* With Gia. She needs me. You can't come. Girl stuff."

"No fair. I'm involved in this, too! I want to come!"

"Ugh, fine. Fine! Just get ready fast. We have to go—now!"

Carla and Matt threw their shoes on in record time and made it downtown without incident. By the time they arrived at *Charmed to Table,* Gia was already there, waiting in her car for them. Carla watched as Gia jumped out of her car and walked over to meet them.

"So?" Carla began. "What happened?"

"Oof." Gia groaned.

"It went that well, huh?"

"Worse," Gia said. "Much, much worse."

"Let's go inside," Matt said, interrupting. "We can talk while we eat."

"Is that all you ever think about?" Carla asked, staring at Matt. "Our friend needs us, and all you can think about is food?"

"Carla, my love, my princess, my baby girl, we are standing *outside* a *restaurant.* The plan was to eat *at* that restaurant. As much as I adore listening to you and Gia discuss her love life, the fact of the matter is that I primarily came along to eat! So, let's compromise and do both... *inside* the restaurant. The one that's literally *right there!*"

Carla rolled her eyes at Matt. "Pardon my husband, Gia. He doesn't know how to function if he isn't stuffing his face with something edible." Carla poked Matt in the ribs, and he feigned being offended, causing a slight grin to grace Gia's expression.

"Watch it, or you won't be experiencing *any* of my 'eating' anytime soon, wifey."

"Okay, okay. Take it easy, you two. You're right, Matt. Let's go eat," Gia said.

"I'm right? Can I get that in writing? I hear it so infrequently around our place." Matt smirked.

"Oh, whatever. You big oaf," Carla said, wrapping her arm around her husband's waist. "I don't know why I put up with you."

"It's because you looooove me... and that whole eating thing."

"Mmhm, something like that, Matty. Something like that."

"On that note," Gia interrupted, "let's go inside before I vomit." Carla and Matt grinned at each other, trying to contain their flirting. Together, the three walked toward the restaurant, with Matt pulling the door open for the two women he was accompanying.

"A table for three, please," Gia told the hostess, who grabbed three menus and walked the group to a table near the back of the dining area.

Charmed to Table was comfortable and inviting. The décor focused on natural elements, including plants, flowers, fruits, and vegetables. However, the breathtaking focal point of the main dining area was a living wall that separated the two sides of the room with paths cut through to allow for entry and exit. The wall featured a variety of herbs and edible plants, and chefs and bartenders would venture out into the main dining area to pick a selection every so often, much to the delight of the restaurant's patrons. Large windows on every side bathed the restaurant in warmth and natural light.

The group arranged themselves at the table, and a waitress quickly appeared.

"Can I take your drink order now, or do you need a few minutes?"

"Drinks now!" Carla declared, grinning. "I'll take a margarita on the rocks. Oh, wait..." Carla's eyes caught the specialty drink menu sitting in the center of the table. "Hang on a sec, let me just—ahh, perfect—make that a pineapple jalapeno margarita!"

"I can tell that gift card isn't going to get us very far here today," Gia said, glancing at the drink prices.

"Eh, whatever. I'll pay the overage," Matt said. "As long as we can order fast. I'm starving!"

"Matty, you're *always* starving. What are you drinking, first?" Carla grinned at her husband, tickling him below the ribcage.

"Hmm, let me see that menu. If you can be fancy, so can I! In honor of our company," Matt gestured at Gia, "I'll try the herb-infused 'old fashioned.'"

"What's in that?" asked Gia.

"I don't even know, but it sounded fancy. Rosemary, I think it said?"

Carla stared at Matt with her eyes wide. "I don't even know who you are anymore. Do you even like old fashioned cocktails?"

"I like whiskey." He chuckled. "Now, Gia, for the love of all things sacred, just order a drink so we can eat!"

"A mojito, please!" Gia announced quickly. Then, inexplicably, her head disappeared as she ducked under the table.

"Did you drop something?" asked Carla, confused.

"Shh!" Gia pressed her finger to her lips, still beneath the table.

"Uh... why am I shh-ing?" Carla's words shifted to a whisper as she inched her head closer to the table.

"By the hostess. Look over by the hostess. He's *talking* to the hostess."

Carla turned her head to the left and saw none other than Ben himself standing beside a stunning, jet-black-haired beauty. Just then, Carla eyed the waitress, standing beside Gia, looking lost. "Oh, you can put those drink orders in. As it turns out, we need a little more time for the food order."

"Why? Why do we need more time?" Matt groaned and face-palmed himself.

"Who's that woman?" Carla began as she pulled Gia upward. "Come up. You have to come up."

"No. I don't. And I don't know. And I don't care."

"Come up right now," Carla said through gritted teeth, tugging harder at Gia until she finally surfaced just in time to lock eyes with Ben as the hostess led him and the mystery woman past their table to the one directly behind.

"Gia!" Ben blurted out. "I... hi. What are you doing down there?"

Gia coughed. "I, uh, I dropped my fork." Ben glanced at her still-empty hands. "Couldn't find it," she quickly added with an uncomfortable shrug. "What are you doing here?"

Ben nearly forgot about the woman at his side as he spoke to Gia. She had his full attention. "I was, uh, I mean, I was going to—"

"*We* were going to be eating lunch. Hi there, nice to meet you. I'm Jen, and you are?" Jen interrupted, batting her eyelashes elegantly as she spoke, which made Carla feel like vomiting. A quick glance at Gia told her that she felt similarly.

"We are," Carla began, "Carla, Matt, and Gia. Old friends of Ben's. Actually, Gia and Ben were *very* close at one time. In fact, hey, why don't you join us?" Carla smirked. "We'd love to catch up on what good old Benny boy has been doing over the past several years—and hours. Wouldn't we, Gia? Matt?"

Gia leaned into Carla and whispered, "Carla, what are you doing? No! Are you crazy?"

Ben was at a loss for words and appeared extremely uncomfortable with the entire situation. "Uh, I don't think that's a very good—"

"We would love to!" Jen jumped in, grinning. "The more the merrier, right? Besides, this looks like it could make for an interesting afternoon. We were hoping for a little entertainment," she said with a chuckle. "I just didn't think it'd be this easy to find." She glanced back and forth between Gia and Ben as if she could read their entire past.

Jen strode over to a nearby table, grabbed two additional place settings, and pulled two chairs to the group's table. "She's certainly not shy," Carla whispered to Matt, who scowled at her.

"Yet again, you couldn't mind your own business?"

Carla groaned as quietly as possible. "I didn't actually think they'd say yes."

Jen plopped herself down at one of the newly added chairs and tugged downward on the belt loop of Ben's jeans, indicating that he should sit. "Seems like you all might have a lot to catch up on if I'm reading the situation correctly," Jen continued, placing a hand on Ben's knee where she was sure Gia would see it.

"Now, the question is, where do we start?" Jen's teasing eyes and tone of voice held a twinge of danger. With each word, she hinted that they were all in trouble—or perhaps only Gia and Ben—without making any actual threats.

"I feel like this was maybe a bad idea," Carla whispered to Matt as quietly as possible.

"Ya think?" he muttered sarcastically, rolling his eyes.

Table for Two

GIA

Chapter 25

GIA STARED AT JEN. Long black hair fell sleekly over her shoulders, neatly swept behind her ears, which boasted a series of small diamond studs climbing the cartilage, adding a slight toughness to her features. A tiny nose ring graced her one nostril, almost unnoticeable. Jen's piercing, dark-lined eyes peered out, sparkling with mischief. Her appearance was desirable in all the ways Gia had always felt she wasn't. Unlike Gia's natural "girl next door" beauty, Jen dripped with sensuality and sex appeal. She was a treat to the senses—from how she smelled to the sound of her voice, confident and self-assured.

How can I compete with that? Gia thought as she tried to process the events of the past few moments. *Wait, I'm not competing. I don't want him. This is only about Aiden. He isn't even supposed to be here right now!* Gia shook her head, trying to focus on the situation at hand. Thankfully, Carla interrupted the awkward silence, trying to make conversation.

"So, uh, Jen... How do you know Ben exactly?"

"Oh, it's the funniest thing," Jen said, squeezing Ben's knee as he squirmed awkwardly in his seat. "We only just met on a dating site this morning. Maybe you've heard of it—*Only Gardeners.*"

Gia squinted and glanced at Ben, then shifted her eyes back to Jen, carefully taking in her appearance and paying particular attention to her pristinely clean, well-manicured fingernails. She tried to hold her tongue, but the words escaped.

"*You* have a garden?"

"Not exactly." Jen smirked. "I have a certain affinity for hard-working men. I was hoping to find someone who is strong and, you know, good with his hands—and low and behold, there was Benji!" Jen threw an exaggerated wink toward Ben, who looked incredibly uncomfortable but jumped into the conversation anyway, trying to save face.

"She—uh, we—uh—we only just started talking... We were both hungry and thought maybe a casual lunch would—"

"Hungry, indeed," Jen interrupted. "No expectations, if you know what I mean." As she spoke, Jen traced her fingertips from Ben's knee to his thigh, causing him to tense up from head to toe. "So, how do you all know each other, anyway? You mentioned you were old friends or something, right?"

"We went to school together," Carla said. "It's complicated."

Matt, who had been silent until then, let out a chuckle. "That's for sure," he said. "Are we still going to eat or...?"

Ignoring Matt's inquiry, Jen continued her line of questioning. "Interesting. I love complicated—and I sense there's more to this story than you've shared. Especially between these two. Am I right?" Jen gestured to Gia and Ben, a teasing smile dancing on the corners of her lips. "I'd love to know more.

After all, I need to know what I'm getting into with Benji Boy here."

Gia couldn't take it any longer. The awkwardness between her and Ben, the meddling of this... this Jen person. It was all too much. She was here to enjoy a meal with her friends, not to be taunted by some high and mighty sex goddess wannabe!

"So, Jen... Okay. You want the scoop? Alright, you asked for it. And so did you," Gia said, glancing at Ben. "So, here it is. Ben is the father of my child. The absentee father. The father who left me to figure it all out, pregnant, alone, and right out of high school. Ben is the man who ditched me for a dream we used to share. *Your Benji boy* is, quite frankly, a dick. So, good luck with that. I think you should leave—both of you. Go enjoy your *no expectations* somewhere else, or at the very least, at your own table. Preferably far away from this one. Ben and I have nothing more to say to each other. And I have even less to say to you. I'd like to enjoy the company of my friends now, if you don't mind."

Carla's jaw dropped, along with Matt's. Jen looked momentarily stunned. And Ben looked absolutely miserable. Gia wasn't one to speak out, and Jen certainly wasn't used to anyone standing up to her. She remained silent for a few seconds, taken aback and still gathering her words.

"Well, then, we'll just be on our way, won't we Benji? There are plenty of *other things* we can do. I'm sure Ben would love to be *eating out* elsewhere with me," Jen said, emphasizing certain words to denote the sexual nature of her comment. However, much of her confidence had clearly dissipated, and she was just going through the motions.

Ben sat at the table, burying his head in his hands. When he finally removed them, Gia saw him wipe a tear from his cheek.

"Jen, I'm sorry, but you should go. I'll go, too—but not together."

Jen scoffed and stared at Ben incredulously. "Seriously? Wow. Just wow. File this under the absolute worst first date ever." She rolled her eyes, stared at the ceiling momentarily, then pushed her chair back and stood up. "Whatever. I'm out of here. You people have issues." She glanced from person to person before storming toward the restaurant exit, leaving Carla, Matt, Gia, and Ben sitting around the table.

Interrupting the awkward silence, their waitress appeared beside them. Not witnessing the previous few moments, she revealed a cheerful, unaffected smile that quickly faded as she took in the expressions around the table. "Uh, are we all ready to order? Oh, or are we waiting on someone?" she stammered, glancing at the empty chair where Jen had been a few moments ago. Ben leaned toward the waitress and whispered something to her. She placed a hand on his shoulder, almost as if she knew him on a more personal level, nodded and took one menu away. Suddenly, Carla's eyes lit up.

"Oh!" she blurted out as she shoved her chair away from the table. "I just remembered! We have—that thing. Right, Matt? That thing I almost forgot about. We have to go right now!" Carla smirked, knowing neither Ben nor Gia would have the audacity to stand up and walk out without placing orders. "So," Carla began, smiling sweetly at the waitress, "it turns out this will only be a table for two now. Sorry for any confusion!"

Matt stared at Carla as she tugged his arm, pulling him away from the table. "But, I—" Matt gazed longingly at the menu still opened before him and rested a hand on his stomach.

"Let's go, Matt. The thing!" Carla pressed. Matt groaned but allowed himself to be pulled toward the exit, knowing it wasn't worth an argument—and that she'd owe him later.

As they approached the door, Carla glanced over her shoulder at Ben and Gia, still staring with mouths agape. "Oh, uh, you can have our drinks. Enjoy!" she called, then shrugged semi-apologetically and walked out the door, pushing her palm against Matt's back to keep him moving.

The Longest Lunch

BEN

Chapter 26

"Uh, we just need a few minutes, please," Ben told the waitress, tapping his menu to indicate they were still deciding, given the chaos that had just ensued. "I'm sorry for the delay, Tara."

The waitress smiled, probably relieved that at least two of the original party of five would remain to leave her a tip. "Of course. I'll be back in a bit," she said, walking away to check in on those dining at nearby tables.

"Gia, I'm so sorry," Ben started. "I didn't know you would be here. I didn't know she would—"

"How do you know her name?" Gia gestured at the waitress, who had moved a couple of tables over to check on other diners.

"What? Tara? Oh—name tag. But, Gia, I had never even met Jen until just now, and it was just a distraction."

"Forget about it. It doesn't even matter," Gia said, picking up the menu and pretending to look at the lunch options. "Let's please just order something small so we can both get out of here."

"Alright," Ben agreed, lifting his menu and eying it thoughtfully. As his eyes scanned the lunch selections, a slight smile formed at the corners of his mouth. He had an idea. "Do you know what you want?"

"Yes," Gia said, closing her menu and placing it on the table. Ben did the same, indicating that they were ready to place their order. The waitress glanced toward them before making her way to the table.

"Looks like you're all set! What can I get you?" she asked, looking inquisitively at Gia.

"I'll have the locally foraged mushroom and wild green goat cheese salad, please," Gia said, tracing the words on the menu with her finger to reiterate her selection to the waitress.

"Excellent choice. Is the house honey balsamic alright? It's made with local honey."

"Perfect," Gia confirmed.

"Anything else to go with that?"

"No. Just a quick and easy salad, thank you."

The waitress nodded, then turned to face Ben. "And for you, sir?" The slight smile that had graced Ben's features a few moments ago morphed into a grin as the waitress put her pen to her pad.

"Oh, let's see here. I'm quite hungry this afternoon." Ben stretched his legs in his chair and leaned back. "I had someone rush out on a breakfast meeting. It was a little stressful, and I lost my appetite this morning. Barely ate a crumb." Ben smirked at Gia. "Gotta make up for that lost meal, don't I?"

The waitress only offered an awkward smile, uncertain what to make of Ben's comments. "Sounds good. What can I get you, then?"

"Well, I think I'll start with some appetizers," Ben began. Gia groaned to herself, catching on to Ben's plan. "Let's do that same salad as the lady ordered to start. But let's add a wood-fired farmer's market pizza—to share, of course. Then, we'll certainly want to try the local artisanal cheese plate and charcuterie board. Is it okay to order the rest of my meal after those apps come out? I still have some decisions to make."

"Of course," the waitress responded, jotting the order onto her pad.

Gia realized Ben would drag this out as long—and expensively—as he possibly could until she agreed to talk to him about Aiden or whatever else he wanted to discuss. Sure, she could stand up and leave, but she felt awkward just walking out of the restaurant after her friends had done it once already!

The waitress walked away to put the order into the kitchen. Gia slid Carla's drink in front of her, claiming possession of the alcohol and hoping it would help her through what promised to be a very long lunch. Ben eyed the old fashioned in front of where Matt had been sitting. "You gonna want that one, too?"

"No. Have at it," Gia scoffed.

"Thanks," Ben said, reaching for the drink and sipping it slowly. "Well, that's certainly... interesting." He took a gulp.

Gia gazed at the ceiling and took a deep breath before allowing herself to speak. "Why are you doing this? What do you want?"

"I want to talk to you without you running out the door. I want to meet Aiden. I want to make you understand why I did what I did. I want—" Ben stopped mid-sentence and took a deep breath and another sip of the drink before him, finding his courage. "I want to try again."

"You what?" asked Gia, flabbergasted. "You want to *try again?* After showing up here and prancing around in front of me with fucking Morticia Adams? You want to *try again?!*"

Ben watched as Gia angrily took a deep breath and tried to

compose herself. He could tell she was attempting to avoid causing another scene like the one in the café earlier.

"Gia, Jen didn't mean anything. I'll say it again: it was just a distraction!"

"A distraction? A distraction from what?"

"From us."

"From us? Ben, there *is* no us. There's you, and there's me. That's it. Separate."

"—but there's Aiden," Ben said quietly, afraid to hear Gia's response.

"Aiden isn't yours. You haven't done a damn thing since his birth—or before it—to earn a right to see him or even know about his life. The only thing you did was knock me up, then run away." Gia buried her face in her hands, trying to keep her rapidly developing tears under wraps. "And how many other *distractions* do you have?" Gia couldn't help but notice that lifelong feeling of '*not enough*' sneaking into her psyche.

"Can we talk about this calmly?" Ben asked. "She was the only other person I'd talked to on that app or anywhere else. I'm not looking to date around. That was just—an unfortunate decision. Listen. We really do need to clear up a few things."

As Ben spoke, the waitress appeared with a tray holding two salads, a cheese plate, and a board of delectable-looking meats, nuts, olives, crackers, and more. She placed a salad in front of each of them and the meats and cheeses in the center of the table, placing a small, empty plate next to each salad so they could share the other items.

"The pizza will be out in just a moment!" the waitress said, trying to ignore that both patrons looked like they were about to burst into tears.

"Thank you," Ben and Gia responded simultaneously. As the waitress returned to the kitchen to fetch their pizza, they glanced up, eyes meeting across the table. Somehow, at that moment, the urge to cry dissipated, and instead, Gia let out a slight chuckle. Then, she couldn't stop.

"Gia?" Ben stared at the woman across from him with a confused expression. Gia's chuckle began to rise like a wave until it became a full-on laugh—a very infectious laugh. Ben wasn't even sure why, but somehow, it overtook him with emotion. He began to laugh uncontrollably in response to Gia's laughter, and by the time the waitress returned with their pizza, both Ben and Gia had tears in their eyes—but this time, it wasn't from crying.

As the waitress attempted to present the pizza to the two cackling diners, they tried to get themselves under control, but every time they managed to stop laughing, one would start up again, beginning the whole process again! Finally, after the waitress left the pizza on the table and walked away shaking her head, Gia and Ben regained their composure.

"What—what was that?" Ben finally asked.

"I have no idea. I just... I just... I don't know what to say or do about this—about any of this—about you or Aiden or anything! I don't even know what to do but laugh at this point. You left us. You abandoned us. We weren't enough to keep you here. And I'm laughing about it. I must be losing my mind."

"I mean, there are certainly worse ways to pass a lunch with an old flame than laughter if you think about it."

"Ben, we aren't even old flames. I don't know what we were. We never even talked about it back then. One minute we were—something—and then you were gone, and we were nothing, and then I had Aiden."

"And your ex-husband."

"You have no right to criticize that. He saved us. Regardless of how we worked out in the end, there's not a moment I'm not thankful that he stepped up to the plate and raised Aiden as his own. I don't know where I'd be right now it Steve hadn't stepped in. There was no difference between how he treated Aiden and his biological children. He's a good man and a good father. We just weren't in love. At least not the type of love you need when trying to make a forever life together."

"I already told you I came back."

"What were you expecting? That Aiden and I would just be there waiting for you to appear at our doorstep, crossing our fingers that you'd return from the middle of the damn Amazon rainforest to rescue us?"

"No, but I didn't expect you to give up on us so quickly."

"So quickly? Ben, it wasn't quick. Maybe it felt that way to you while you were off galivanting on your Brazilian adventures, but I faced a pregnancy, the birth of my first child, and a new baby in that period. It felt like a lifetime for me. My dreams came crashing down, and I had to re-write them—every last one of them—without you in them."

"I wanted to be in them. I just realized it too late, is all."

"And now that you're back, you think it's just something we can dive back into headfirst? Being together? It's complicated now."

"How is it any more complicated now than it was before? We are both single. I want to be in Aiden's life. We could try."

"I don't *want* to try. I don't want to go through it again. I knew I didn't love my ex-husband the way I should have to commit to a lifetime together—but I also knew he wouldn't ever be able to break me like you did. I stayed with him *because* he didn't have the power to crush me. I'm not opening myself up to that again."

"Then you're going to have a pretty sad life," Ben muttered. "Trust me."

Dessert

GIA

Chapter 27

"WHAT RIGHT DO you have to tell me that I'm going to have a sad life? I have everything that I need. I have my kids, my house, and my garden. Eat." Gia gestured to the food sitting untouched on the table, hoping they could eat the multitude of appetizers, ask for the bill, and call it quits on the lunch.

"I know that even in Brazil, following my dreams, doing exactly what I wanted to do, I never felt as complete as I did when I was with you. I came back to tell you I needed you with me. Here, there, wherever."

Gia rolled her eyes. "Timing is everything, my friend. Speaking of which, your pull-out timing *sucks*. I've been wanting to tell you that for years."

"Apparently," Ben chuckled. "Gia, let me meet Aiden. Let's see how it goes. You can tell him I'm just a family friend or something."

"He isn't stupid, Ben. And he isn't five, either. He looks *exactly* like you."

"I mean, if he figures it out, he figures it out, right?"

"No. Not right. It's not that simple. Maybe this is something Aiden and I should have talked about long ago, but we didn't. I never knew how to bring it up. First, I thought he was too young, then I didn't want him to feel different from his siblings—and I can't just spring something like this on him now or let him 'figure it out' after seeing you."

Ben shrugged. "Listen, Gia... Let me take you out on a date. A real date. We won't talk about the past or Aiden at all. It'll be just two people getting to know each other and seeing if we still click like we once did."

"It's not that simple."

"It could be."

"Please, just eat," Gia urged, sticking her fork into her salad and shoving the first bite since it'd been placed in front of her into her mouth. Her eyes opened wide. "Oh, wow! That's amazing. Taste that!"

Ben bit into a forkful of salad and began chewing. "Yeah... that's definitely delicious. Let's try the pizza," he suggested, pleased with an opportunity to change the subject and return to more casual conversation. Gia nodded and grabbed a slice of the small gourmet pizza, raising it to her lips and taking a bite before putting it down on the small plate in front of her.

"Yeah, I'll certainly be returning here to try the rest of the menu," Gia said. "I'd have so many ideas for a place like this!"

"I've got news for you: if you refuse to see me for another date, I intend to order the menu in its entirety today—over a prolonged period. And eat very, very slowly."

"Fine, Ben! One more date. One." Gia groaned. *Well, he's persistent. I'll give him that much.*

"One *more* date? Does that mean that this counts as a date, too? Ooh, do we get to kiss?" Ben asked playfully, the corners of his eyes crinkling with his smile.

"Ben..." Gia started.

"Okay, sorry. I'm done. One is all I need!" A wider grin spread across Ben's face.

Please don't let me regret this, thought Gia. "I just don't see how we can get through an entire night completely disregarding the past—which, I'll remind you, flows straight through to the present in the form of a little boy named Aiden. You can't 'get to know' me without learning about Aiden."

"Don't worry about that. Just let me handle the details. Besides, I *want* to learn about Aiden. I just don't want to fight with you over it."

For the next several minutes, the topic of conversation shifted back to the food. Ben and Gia continued their meal, sampling the meats and cheeses and discussing which they liked best and what else they wanted to try from the entrée section of the menu. Meanwhile, Gia pointed out different ways she could re-imagine the courses using her personal garden's produce.

"Speaking of your garden, how's it doing this year?" asked Ben, landing on a topic he knew would be agreeable to both of them, and that didn't pose much of a fight risk—or a flight risk, given how their earlier morning interactions had gone.

"Not bad, honestly. This year, I tried a few experiments with containers versus in-ground plantings and some new companion gardening and integrated pest management plans. Most of them seem to be working well! The pollinator garden is gorgeous, pulling more bees and butterflies than ever. I even have a few hummingbirds coming around. The best part is that it's all native species, so it's pretty self-sufficient! It takes so little effort compared to the other garden areas."

"That's incredible. I'd love to see it. I wish you'd show me."

"Let's get through this meal and our first official date with no more yelling or tears—then we'll see."

"Fair enough."

"Ben." Gia paused to take a deep breath.

"Yeah?"

"What are your actual plans? Are you staying around here or —" Gia's voice trailed off as she got lost in thought, wondering if all this emotional upheaval was for nothing.

"It depends," admitted Ben.

"On what?"

"On you." Ben reached across the table and wrapped his hand around Gia's, pulling it toward an empty space in the center of the table and holding it. "I'm only here for you. I have a big project in the works here, but its success depends on a few key factors."

Gia shifted her eyes down, uncertain what to say or do, but allowed him to hold her hand. His touch still sent a shiver down her spine, a fact she refused to admit out loud.

Slowly, Gia shifted her gaze upward until she made eye contact with Ben. He really had grown up to be quite handsome. She couldn't help but notice the difference. He was no longer a boy. He was a man, and she wondered what else had changed about him despite her efforts to keep her thoughts pure. Her eyes wandered to his broad shoulders and chest, lingering there until the waitress reappeared.

"How is everything?" she asked, clearly pleased that emotions seemed predominantly positive at the table—happy customers, bigger tip!

"Oh, it's wonderful. Delicious, thank you," Gia said, shaking off her wandering thoughts.

"Everything is great," added Ben.

"Can I get you some entrees?"

"Actually," Gia jumped in, "I think we both ate so much of the appetizers that we may be ready to jump straight to dessert and save the other options for another time."

Ben smiled. He knew Gia loved sweets, and as long as she wasn't complaining about staying for another course, he saw it as a good sign. "Works for me," he said. "We'll take a dessert menu when you have a minute."

"Of course," the waitress said, walking away for a moment and returning with two dessert menus.

"This all sounds incredible," breathed Gia. "This place is my new 'go-to' for, well, for everything! Local honey-lavender ice cream, fruit galette, fresh zucchini cupcakes, rhubarb crumble over vanilla ice cream—what more could a garden lover ask for?"

"Seriously. I can't decide. Let's just order all of it and sample the goods," Ben suggested, grinning.

"Ben, that's going to be way too much money. My gift card isn't for *that* much! Single mom, multiple kids, remember?"

"I didn't even know you had a gift card." Ben chuckled. "I was going to say it was my treat, but... now you can pay for part with your gift card, and I'll pay the overage to keep things fair."

"If we order that whole dessert menu, on top of all the drinks and apps, you'll lose out on that deal... it's not going to be an even split by any stretch."

"You know what... I changed my mind. Hang onto that gift card. You'll want to return if you love this place as much as you say. This time is my treat! I'd say I owe it to you at this point."

"Ya think?" Gia said, rolling her eyes but secretly hiding a smile.

When the waitress returned to take their order, her jaw dropped in surprise when Ben informed her that they wanted everything on the dessert menu, but she didn't say anything. Their visit to the restaurant hadn't exactly been by the book so far, so why question it now? She took the order back to the kitchen, and the two fell back into garden talk inspired by the multitude of food ideas Gia had gained from the meal and the different menu options.

Gia was surprised by the level of comfort they easily fell into, chatting without much effort until the desserts began to pour out from the kitchen. They arrived two at a time, with Gia and Ben each sampling a small amount from each, then pushing them to the center of the table and awaiting the next arrivals. They planned to try to finish anything frozen first so they could split up and take home the leftovers when they were too full to eat another bite!

Gia and Ben were shocked by how little remained at the end of their dessert sampling. They'd eaten *so* much that they needed several minutes to digest before even considering paying the bill and leaving. Gia realized that may also have been an excuse to make the meal last just a bit longer! Once they'd stopped arguing, it really had been a fantastic meal.

When they couldn't think of any excuses to stay and the bill was placed on the table, Ben grabbed it before Gia could see the balance. He stood up, walked over to the waitress with the bill and his wallet, and whispered something in her ear. They both laughed, and Ben shook the waitress's hand before returning to the table. As he walked over, Gia thought she noticed Ben glance down at his phone and furrow his brow in concern, but perhaps she had imagined it.

"All set!" Ben said.

"How much?"

"Doesn't matter."

"Ben, tell me."

"Nope! My treat. Consider it my thank you for the opportunity to spend a thoroughly enjoyable meal with the perfect company. One that started a little iffy, I might add. Honestly, I don't think that could have gone better if I'd planned it." He smirked. "By the way, you take the leftovers. I'm watching my figure."

CARLA

"WHY HASN'T SHE CALLED YET?!" Carla asked. "There's no way they could still be eating lunch." Carla pressed her nose against the glass of her living room window, gazing at the house next door. "Her car isn't in the driveway. She's been gone all afternoon!"

"Carla, my love, my treasure, chill out and mind your own damn business," Matt said from the couch as he took a swig from his beer.

"What if they killed each other?!"

"Possible. But highly improbable."

"I mean... she could bury his body so easily! You know, plant some sort of rare, endangered species over it so no one could ever dig it up!"

"You spend way too much time on the internet."

"Maybe—but that doesn't make it any less true. Oh! Oh, she's pulling in! Matt, she's pulling in the driveway!"

Matt took another long drink, chuckling. "Oh, goody."

"Hush, Matty. You're just as invested in this situation as I am. You're just hiding it to be all manly man-ish. We both know you're as much of a meddler at heart as I am!" Carla walked away from the window and wrapped her arms around Matt from behind, kissing him on the head.

"No way. But, just out of curiosity, how long will you wait before you go over there and get the scoop?" Matt tilted his head backward to grin at his wife. "I want to know when I'll have a few minutes to sneak back onto my *Only Gardeners* account." Matt gave Carla an exaggerated wink and grinned.

"Not funny, Mister. I figure I'll give her a half hour or so. I don't want to make it obvious that I was waiting on her."

"Oh, right, because she won't already know you've been staring out the window since the moment we got back from the restaurant, just waiting to pounce. Discretion has never been your strong suit."

Carla laughed. "Whatever, Matt. She loves me for me. Screw it. You're right. I'm going over now."

"That's my girl! See if she has any leftovers that she wants to donate to the Matt fund."

"Do you ever think about anything but food?"

"Sometimes," Matt started. "But we already did that."

Carla rolled her eyes, pulled on a pair of slip-on canvas shoes and walked toward the back door. "Answer your phone if I call—we may need you to help dig," she said. Matt's face took on a perplexed expression until he finally gave in and questioned her.

"Dig what?"

"Shallow grave?"

"You're insane. Go. See friend. Now." Matt waved Carla off,

sending her out the door, down the back steps, and toward the fence at a trot.

Carla pulled the broken fence rail aside and peered into Gia's backyard, listening before she made any sound, trying to gauge the situation. She heard Gia's voice clear as day, and it was— singing! *Well, I don't see any shovels. That's a good sign,* Carla thought, allowing a slight giggle to emerge.

"Carla?" The singing stopped, and Gia's voice rose between two raised beds in the garden area.

Ooh, busted.

"Oh, hi, Gia," Carla stammered. "How... uh... how are things?" Carla began pacing toward the garden with long strides, trying to appear nonchalant.

"Things are—thingy!" Gia responded, intentionally avoiding the topic she knew Carla was there to discuss.

"Would you care to elaborate on that?" Carla smirked at her friend, prying for information.

"Hmm, nope. I think 'thingy' pretty much sums it up!"

"Gia! You tell me immediately how your date with Ben went, or I'll never speak to you again!"

"We both know that's a lie. It would kill you to stop speaking to me before you heard the gossip." Gia grinned at Carla, tugging a piece of her hair gently.

"Regardless. Tell me!"

"Well, first of all, it wasn't a date—just so we're clear. It was a forced lunch."

"Semantics. How was your forced lunch?"

"It was delicious, thanks. *Charmed to Table* is right up my alley. Amazing food, wonderful service, top-notch!" Carla squirmed in her chair as Gia continued about the restaurant's quality. "Great cocktails, fabulous desserts, delic—"

"Wait. Desserts? You two made it to dessert by choice? And no one shed any tears—or blood?" Carla asked.

"We did, indeed." Finally, Gia began to spill the details of their lunch. She summarized the events from the past several hours, from their laughter fit to the more serious discussions. Carla listened as she spoke until only one question remained.

"And after?"

"After what?"

"After the date—I mean, the meal, the lunch, forced lunch, whatever—did you kiss? You said he wanted to take you on a real date. Did you make plans?"

"No, for your information, we didn't kiss. And I'm not telling you anything else. I want to see how it goes before I rattle on about something that isn't even a thing."

"First off, yet. It isn't a thing—*yet*. Second, so you *did* make plans! You *have* to tell me where he's taking you! That's all I'll ask for now, I promise."

"Carla, I don't *have* to do anything. And you, my dear friend, have done *enough* already. Back off! Oh, but first, follow me to the kitchen. I have leftovers for you—or Matt—or whoever wants them. I can't eat another bite, and these desserts won't taste nearly as good tomorrow or even later today. Farm-to-table is always best eaten fresh."

"Ahh, Matt told me to ask if you had anything." Carla grinned. "I forgot."

"At least one of us is looking out for your husband's bottomless pit of a stomach," Gia said with a slight chuckle.

"You feed him; I make him do cardio." Carla made a raunchy motion with her hips, moving them in and out.

"Aaaand, changing the subject... Kitchen. Now. Let's go."

Gia led the way past several tall trellises with sugar snap pea vines rising up and throughout, then ducked slightly under a curved piece of wire fencing she had placed over the walkway. Between the spring and the start of the summer, climbing flowers in various bright hues had wrapped their way around the wires, creating a breathtakingly beautiful—and delectably scented— garden tunnel. It was one of her favorite floral features this year, and her children loved running through one end and out the other. Even better, she had done it on a whim when she realized she had extra materials available after a repair to the dog's fenced area.

Having almost run out of gardening space in the existing beds, growing *up* became one of her favorite new hobbies! Despite the importance of the lessons the kids learned almost daily in her garden, Gia always wanted to ensure her children had at least some free space in the yard for running and playing. She devised several brilliant ways to keep the garden condensed while increasing her yearly yields. Still, someday, Gia hoped to grow on a larger scale with a bigger purpose than feeding her family. She had an endless array of ever-building ideas in her mind. Seeing the incredible farm-to-table options available at *Charmed to Table* kickstarted that desire once again.

Gia and Carla entered the kitchen, and Gia pulled out five separate containers of dessert leftovers.

"Jeez, Gia. What'd you do? Order the whole menu?" Carla asked, causing Gia to laugh out loud. "Oh my God, you did. You guys actually did! I guess it *did* go well."

"Shush. Take the food to your spouse. We'll catch up on the rest later."

"Gia, this is torture! I need more details!"

"And, perhaps, in time, you'll get them. But, for now, I'm not jinxing this by talking about it. It's messy enough as it is. I won't get my hopes up that anything will come from it, but I also won't destroy it by running my mouth before I've given it a chance."

"Given what, exactly, a chance? Ben? A relationship? Something along those lines?"

"Goodbye, Carla!" Gia gently pushed Carla toward the door, opening it for her and ushering her back to the garden, then waving her off toward the fence. "Say hey to Matt for me and tell him to enjoy the food."

Carla groaned and headed through the gap in the fence toward her own house, muttering something inaudible under her breath.

When Gia heard Carla's deck door slam shut, she grabbed her

phone, wandered back inside to her living room, and sat on the couch, resting her feet on the matching ottoman. She needed to regroup and think things over before her children returned home from their father's house. She also wanted to check her messages. Gia had given Ben her cell phone number earlier to avoid the need for any further *Only Gardeners* interactions, but she'd left it on the patio to keep it dry while handling her garden chores. Having already destroyed several phones in the garden over the years, she'd learned her lesson the hard way.

Gia turned on the screen on her phone and immediately noticed the text message notification icon at the top of the screen. She sucked in a breath of air and swiped down with a shaky finger to read the detailed notification and phone number information —*Ben.*

A "Wealth" of Information

BEN

BEN SAT in his armchair in the reclined position, feet up. It had undoubtedly been an eventful day, and he was fully prepared to remain in the relative safety of his apartment for the remainder of the afternoon. He stretched his legs outward and reached for the TV remote, placing it on the extra wide arm on the side of his chair. Upon reaching into his pocket to remove his wallet and phone, his fingers caught on a piece of paper—no, a slightly crumpled napkin. Ben pulled it out, turned it around and peered at it as if it would bite him. *Charmed to Table* was written above the restaurant's logo, with Gia's phone number just below.

Ben glanced at the napkin again and felt his chest tighten with anxiety. He wanted to text her, but his fingers didn't move.

He felt frozen. *Why am I being such a wuss? What's wrong with reaching out to a woman after spending a lovely afternoon together —even if we didn't mean to spend it together?* Ben shrugged in response to his own question. "Nothing," he finally said aloud. "Absolutely nothing!"

He carefully typed the digits from the napkin into his phone, storing the number and double-checking it before he began crafting his greeting:

Hey Gia, it's Ben. I hope you enjoyed our lunch today. I'm really looking forward to the rare plant show at the botanical garden this week—I hope you are, too.

Ben slapped his hand over his forehead. "This sounds stupid," he muttered, erasing the message and starting over:

Hey there, Gia. Ben here. It was nice seeing you—especially when we weren't yelling at each other. Are we still on for the rare plants on Wednesday?

Ben read the message, shaking his head. *Ugh. Trying too hard. Ben, this isn't rocket science,* he thought. *Okay, one more try...*

Hi Gia, it's Ben. I enjoyed lunch and hope you did as well. Are we still on to visit the botanical garden for the rare plant show? Let me know if Wednesday is still okay. I know scheduling can be challenging with the kids.

"That'll have to do." He hoped bringing up scheduling would show her he knew what he would be getting into if they started dating. He hit send, hoping for a rapid reply. No such luck. An hour passed, and his message sat unread. Ben couldn't help but wonder if Gia had given him a fake number or whether she was just ignoring him to play it cool or—the worst—ghosting him entirely. He rapidly moved his head back and forth, trying to shake it off, then placed his phone in his lap and closed his eyes. *What will be will be, I guess.*

He awoke to his phone vibrating on his lap, causing him to jump, blinking in surprise as he got his bearings. He swiped his screen to open his notifications. Two messages. He read the first, an angry expression morphing his features. *Jen.*

Hey Benji, what was up with that little display? She's not even a quarter of the woman I am. Let's meet up for some fun.

Jesus Christ, Ben thought. *She's crazy.*

Jen: I'm not interested. Please stop texting me. I have things to work out in my life right now. I'm sorry for any confusion I may have caused.

Ben rolled his eyes as he hit send. He'd seen enough crazy from Jen. His frown disappeared as he realized the other message was from Gia! Ben couldn't hide his excitement, but no one was around to judge him, anyway. He began to read:

Hey. Sorry for the delayed response. I was in the garden. I'm in for Wednesday. Just let me know where and when you want to meet.

Matt grinned from ear to ear, letting the positive-sounding response sink in. A real date. She was interested in meeting him for an actual date, one they'd planned, not one they'd been trapped in. Ben couldn't help but wonder if this was a second chance at getting something back that he thought he'd lost a long time ago—in what felt like another lifetime.

For Ben's entire adult life, Gia had been the one who got away. From the moment he returned from Brazil and found her married to another man and raising a newborn—his newborn—he'd felt a deep sense of loss. It was a nagging pain that stayed with him wherever he went and whatever he did. It wasn't jealousy. It was something more significant.

He'd made the biggest mistake of his life, realized it too late, and was unable to do anything about it. Nothing Ben tried or accomplished could fill the gap in his world that losing Gia had created, but he knew he couldn't just upturn the life she'd created to survive the mess he'd left her in. So, he went back. He finished his commitment with *World Corps* in Brazil and just kept going. His travels went much further than South America. He spent years searching for something to replace Gia with—and he never found it. Not in Borneo, Cameroon, Australia, the Democratic Republic of Congo, or anywhere else.

What he did find, however, was an unexpected fortune.

When he realized he needed a break, he declared himself "retired." He returned to his hometown finding the town and himself changed in many ways, but the same in others. It didn't take long for him to discreetly ask around town about Gia, quickly learning she had moved into a quiet, pretty neighborhood—and, interestingly—that she had gotten divorced relatively recently.

Having succeeded in tourism already, Ben didn't take long to realize that he wanted to continue to work in the service industry in a way that connected several of his other interests. Lucky for him, two storefronts had gone up for sale downtown. A coffee-lover from birth, Ben didn't think twice about purchasing the *Café on Main* and re-branding it as *Cold Brew: The Café on Main*.

Then, when a nearby restaurant was listed, Ben didn't bat an eye as he offered the sellers, locals for their entire lives, straight cash—and significantly more than they had asked for. *Charmed to Table* became his pet project, a farm-to-table restaurant focused on gourmet local and regional food items—always fresh and of the highest quality. With a constantly shifting menu based on what was in-season at the time, it supported local farms and the broader community. Ben had several other ideas for the space, like community cooking and gardening classes, food distributions for those with limited access or funds for food, and more. He had other dreams for *Charmed to Table* as well, but they were on hold until he saw how things panned out with Gia—if she even remembered he existed.

Returning with money hadn't been a goal when Ben left his hometown, but it sure made things easier as he built and branded the businesses. As they say, it takes money to make money, and both the café and the restaurant were doing quite well already with the funds he'd poured into advertising, staffing, and branding! He had high hopes they would continue to do so—and even higher hopes for other parts of his life.

Ben glanced at his phone again, mentally preparing to respond to Gia's text, and then he started typing.

B: *Can I pick you up? I think it would just make things easier if we headed there together. If not, no worries. I leave it up to you. If so, Wednesday at 9 am?*

G: *Sure, that works. I'll text you the address to use for GPS in a separate message.*

Part of Ben was concerned that if they traveled together, they'd be stuck together. Their first two interactions had involved Gia running away from him, and despite his high hopes that this one would end differently, he felt that with those odds, there was still slight cause for concern. But Ben pushed the thought from his mind, trying to focus on the success of their last unexpected outing instead.

His phone vibrated again, this time with a message containing Gia's address and confirmation of the time for pickup. *Excellent,* Ben thought. *And terrifying.*

Wardrobe

~~~

GIA

THE TIME FOLLOWING Ben and Gia's impromptu lunch date
passed quickly. The long days but short years of motherhood
kept her busy with the children—feeding them, meeting their
needs, getting them ready for school, serving as a chauffeur to
transport them here and there, forcing them to do their homework, and arguing with them over screen time and proper use of
the internet. When she was with her kids, they were her priority.
Even when they weren't with her, most of her activities centered
around making money to meet the growing expense of their
activities, food intake, and so on.

In addition, there was a garden to tend to, crops to harvest,
and food to prep. Then, there were work responsibilities. Gia was

grateful that she was self-employed and could work on her own terms—as long as she met her client's deadlines. It wasn't a particularly lucrative career, nor her "dream job," but she liked that her various freelance projects allowed her to learn a great deal on various topics, and the flexibility she needed to care for her children.

Gia chatted with Ben by text here and there, but it was predominantly casual and surface-level. Nothing deep or overwhelmingly flirty. If her history with Ben had taught her anything, it was to keep her guard up. Her emotional walls were high and constructed of impenetrable material, and she had every intention of keeping it that way! Even her ex-husband could not break down her barriers, which she admitted may have been part of the cause of their eventual demise as a married couple. She couldn't open up to him, and so, however right or wrong it may have been, he sought emotional connections elsewhere—first in the text messages and later in the arms of a co-worker!

What Gia found the most interesting was how easily she healed from the betrayal. Of course, her life was flipped upside down for a while, and her heart ached for what once was. But after the emotional upheaval following the initial blow of discovering his extramarital affair, she talked to a therapist for a while, then simply got on with her life. If she was being honest, Ben had hurt her heart significantly more than her husband cheating on her, a realization that terrified Gia, given the nature of her and Ben's short, unlabeled relationship. She knew he held a certain inexplicable power over her heart, and the idea that she was inviting him back into her life—even if it worked out to be just as a father figure to Aiden—was frightening.

She shook off reminders of that fear whenever they tried to creep into her mind simply by following her daily routine. However, by Tuesday night, the evening before their morning date, Gia frantically pulled clothes from her closet again as she tried to find the perfect date outfit. Casual enough for a stroll through the botanical garden, but she wanted to exude the confidence of a grown woman—not a scared girl—who had her life together.

"No," she said aloud, tossing a long, gray knit sweater to the floor. "Too grandma-ish." She placed her fingers against her temples and rotated them in frustration to ease the slight tension headache she felt developing. "Nope, too ugly." She rolled her eyes at the high-necked top she'd pulled out next. "This isn't working. I give up!" Gia slammed her closet door shut, leaving a mess of clothes on the floor.

She sat on her bed and began typing furiously into her phone, texting Carla.

G: *I need to come over. No clothes.*

C: *YES! Makeover!*

G: *No. Just clothes.*

C: *Come over. The door is open.*

G: *Be right there.*

Gia grabbed a pair of flip-flops and threw them on her feet as she walked out the door toward Carla's. She climbed the deck stairs two at a time and entered from the patio.

"Carla?" she called as she walked into the house.

"Upstairs! Come up!"

Once upstairs, Gia glanced at Carla's bed, piled high with different outfit pairings, awaiting Gia's review. "Wow. You work fast!"

"You know this is my jam! Try this first," Carla said, holding up a low-cut, slinky black top.

"Nope. No way. I'm going to the botanical garden, not the nightclub!"

"Ooh! You just revealed a secret! I didn't know where you were going because you didn't *tell* me when I asked the other day. Ugh, fine, then you pick one!" Carla rolled her eyes at her friend, gesturing to the bed.

"No... No... Nope. Carla, all of these look like I belong in a strip club!" Gia tossed a short, sequined dress aside. "This isn't what I'm going for." She walked over to the closet and pushed hanger after hanger aside, examining its contents.

"Ooh!" Gia blurted out. "This... just might work!" Gia held up the bottom of a soft, floral-patterned wrap dress, her eyes widening. "I've never seen you wear this!"

"It's not really my style. I actually forgot I even owned that. If you want it, you can have it. Here—leggings!"

Gia pulled the dress off the hanger and lifted it over her head before donning the leggings and peering into the mirror on the back of the closet door. The dress hugged Gia's curves perfectly, with a neckline cut just low enough to add a touch of sex appeal without looking like she was trying too hard.

"Perfect!" she exclaimed.

"Well, it wouldn't have been my first choice—but then again, not everyone can have my extraordinarily fabulous sense of style," Carla said with a shrug. "It looks amazing on you, anyway." Carla gave her friend's shoulder a comforting squeeze. "It's very you. Are you excited?"

"Nervous," Gia admitted. "And I don't even know why."

"I mean, it's kind of a big deal... recently single, going out with your son's father. There are so many what-ifs... or could-be's there."

"Thanks for the reminder," Gia said sarcastically. "Really helps calm me down."

"Sorry. You know I'm not one for subtlety," Carla said with a chuckle.

"You can say that again!" Gia began removing the borrowed clothes, folding them carefully to avoid causing any wrinkles that would frustrate her the following day. "Do you think he's nervous, too?"

"I have no doubt about it."

Ben

"My clothes suck! They all suck! They're all only good for

trekking through the rainforest or attending a business meeting with resort executives—there are no date clothes!" Ben spoke to himself as he tore his wardrobe apart in search of something appropriate for his date the next day. He wondered if Gia was nervous, too. He couldn't imagine her struggling with an outfit. She could wear a garbage bag and still look breathtaking, as far as he was concerned.

"That's it," Ben grumbled. "This isn't working!" He threw the pants he held onto the bed, already strewn with other items, and grabbed his keys off the nightstand. "I'm going shopping." When he reached his car, he hopped in and pushed the button on the ignition. Noticing the beautiful day, he put the top of the convertible down before reversing out of his parking space. Ben wasn't one for buying flashy things or showing off. He liked to remain under the radar and keep things simple. In fact, the car had been his one and only 'frivolous' purchase after he returned home to an overflowing bank account—and he didn't regret it. Going for a drive, top-down, sun shining, became his primary source of therapy. His way of coping when life became over-whelming.

As he reached the end of the block, he turned the steering wheel right and eased the car onto the main road. "Where to go, where to go?" Ben questioned aloud. "Main Street. Plenty of options there." He headed toward Main Street, planning to stop into his shop for a coffee before he hit the block with several men's clothing stores in a row. By the time he reached *Cold Brew,* he felt much calmer. The drive had worked wonders on his nerves and cleared his mind.

"Hey there, Morgan," Ben said to the barista behind the counter. "Just a large Brazilian brew coffee, please." The barista gave him her biggest smile. By all accounts, Ben was an excellent boss. He had quickly earned the respect of the shop's staff— partly by keeping all the previous café workers on and giving them each a substantial raise.

"Coming right up! Set up as usual?" she asked, walking over

to the extensive coffee brewing system arranged against the back wall.

"Yep, and I'll take that to go," Ben added, moving to the other end of the counter to await his beverage. Within minutes, he held a hot cup of strong coffee fixed just as he liked it. The bold flavor reminded him of rainforest mornings, waking up early to start the day with a few moments of peace. Sipping the coffee felt like a brief journey into another life—one he had been prepared to give up if it meant he could have a relationship with Gia and get to know his son.

Ben's successes in the rainforest translated well to his work back in the states. His research and on-site experience with rain-forest ecosystems and sustainable coffee farming and develop-ment enabled him to master a system that paired tourism with carefully coordinated environmental research and ecological preservation of the rainforest. After opening his first resort—a two-hut compound with a staff consisting of one cook, a house-keeper, and several scientists hosting a few guests per week, interest—and investors—began to pour in. After *Amazonas* magazine published an article on the eco-resort, Ben's expertise was in high demand, with tourism executives reaching out daily, hoping to ride the coattails of his highly successful tourism endeavor.

Ben's role shifted unexpectedly from eco-resort manager to world traveler and consultant extraordinaire—and his experience came with a hefty price tag that large resorts were all too happy to pay as environmental concerns and interest in the growing eco-tourism field expanded. By the time things slowed down in the industry, Ben had stockpiled millions without realizing it. He was merely following his dream to travel, see the world, make a differ-ence, and escape the poor decisions that led to him losing Gia and Aiden and all that could have been.

His love for strong, bold coffee was further fueled during his travels, allowing him to network and establish connections neces-sary to acquire fair-trade coffee from his eco-tourism resorts worldwide, generating income for them and yielding high-quality products for the café. The café was his global support endeavor. It tied him to an essential part of his past and provided an ever-present reminder of where he'd been and what he'd learned along the way.

"Thanks a lot!" Ben told the staff member, placing a twenty-dollar bill into the tip jar. Ben hadn't used his fortune to buy anything crazy—except his vehicle, the café, and the restaurant, but they were already turning a profit—so he liked to use his money to thank those around him for their efforts. After all, it was the service industry, and money was an excellent motivator to ensure his staff continued to provide outstanding service!

Ben gave a quick wave and made his way out of the café and toward the clothing stores on foot. Out of the corner of his eye, he could have sworn he saw a tall woman with long, black hair slink into one of the nearby shops. *Jen? No. Couldn't be.*

Matt's Makeover

BEN

Chapter 31

WHEN BEN ARRIVED at the line of clothing stores on Main Street, he scanned them, glancing into the store windows to see which would best fit what he was looking to purchase. *Too fancy. Too casual. Too young. Too—oh, perfect!*

Ben's eyes caught on a store featuring a group of mannequins donning nice-looking jeans and slacks with stylish but casual button-down shirts. He walked over to the storefront and pulled the door open, stepping inside and looking around. As he gazed at the variety of options before him, he began pulling the items he liked best from their respective locations, creating a try-on pile. Ordinarily, Ben wasn't one to try on clothes, but this was a special occasion.

Satisfied with what he held, he walked toward the fitting room in the rear of the store, where he was surprised by the sound of his name.

"Ben! Nice to see you again—under potentially less awkward circumstances," Matt's voice bellowed confidently from behind, reminding Ben that the last time they'd seen each other was when he showed up to *Charmed to Table* with Jen. "What brings you here? I'm escaping my wife and Gia's little makeover session, which, for some reason, is occurring at my house."

It took Ben a moment to process an answer, especially after the mention of Gia. "Uh, clothes?" he said. "An outfit. Nothing I have is—date appropriate." Ben realized that attempting to hide the fact that he was shopping for clothes for his date with Gia would be a lost cause.

Matt gave Ben a knowing grin. "Ahh, the irony. Need some help making a choice?" he asked. "I'm known for my exquisite sense of manly style, you know. Might as well do a makeover, too."

Ben shrugged, uncertain, but nodded in agreement, realizing he could use the help. "Okay, you know what? Sure. This isn't exactly my area of expertise. I've been traipsing around the jungle for years. My apparel wasn't exactly high on the list of things people cared about in my line of work."

Despite Ben's foray into the business side of the tourism and travel industry, most of his clothes had been selected *for* him when he set foot out of the forest. Even so, Ben knew full well he could have shown up to any of his business meetings in full jungle trekking gear—or even dressed as a tribal shaman—and it would have only added to the allure of his eco-resort concept.

"Alright, first off... No. Put that shit back, bro," Matt said, assessing the clothes pile in Ben's hands before placing them on the rack for unwanted items in the entry to the fitting room.

"But I liked those."

"No. You didn't. Trust me. You really, really didn't." Matt rolled his eyes and clucked his tongue against his teeth, shaking his head. "Ahh, young grasshopper... it's time you learned the ways of the modern man's wardrobe!"

"I don't think Gia—"

"Shhh," Matt interrupted, placing a finger against his lips. He glanced at Ben, assessing his size by eye, then looked down at the pile of clothes he had selected for himself to try on. He tossed a pair of dark wash, bootcut jeans at Ben, followed by a tight-fitting, dark gray, ribbed sweater. "We are probably around the same size. Try these."

Ben stared at the clothes he was now holding. He couldn't hide the wince that formed across his features. The pants weren't bad, but the shirt was definitely not his style. "Matt, I appreciate it, but this isn't really my—"

"Put... on... the... clothes. Then, if you don't like how they look, I promise you can kick me out of this fitting room and carry on with your last-era shopping spree. I'll leave you alone with your... taste." Matt placed a hand on Ben's back and gave him a gentle shove into the fitting room stall before plopping down on the sofa, waiting for him to emerge again.

Ben sighed, resigned to his fate. At least if he hated the clothes once they were on, Matt would drop the subject and disappear. Ben hoped, anyway. He pulled off his clothing and stepped into the dark jeans. *Not bad,* he thought. *Well, at least I can tell Matt I'm on board with the pants.* Then, he pulled the sweater over his head, tugging it down over his torso once his arms were entirely in the shirt. It was tighter than most of the clothes he was used to wearing, but when he looked in the mirror, he was pleasantly surprised that he didn't hate it.

He was even willing to admit it looked good. Ben had poured a great deal of physical labor in while working in the jungle, and it showed. He wasn't used to wearing clothing that highlighted his 'assets,' particularly his well-formed chest muscles and broad shoulders. The top Matt selected did it well. He looked like he spent *way* more time lifting weights at the gym than he actually did.

"What do you think?" Matt's voice interrupted Ben's assessment of the clothes now that they were on his body.

"I... I admit that this was a good choice—and that I probably have no idea what I'm talking about when it comes to men's apparel. Fashion was never really my thing."

"Score! Let me see how they look."

Ben opened the door to the fitting room, revealing the outfit he'd selected. "Damn! You're ripped! You'd never even have known it. You need to show that off, man!"

"Grab some other stuff for me?" Ben asked, chuckling. "Might as well see what else you come up with!"

"Hell yeah!" Matt said. Rather than returning to the front of the store, Matt handed Ben the rest of the clothes he had originally brought back to try on himself. "Here. See how far this takes you! Feeling wealthy?" Ben closed the fitting room door, ignoring the question to avoid discussing his true financial circumstances.

Sharing that information with Matt and having it get back to Gia wasn't something he was prepared to do. He wanted to win her back for love or to have a relationship with Aiden, but not for money. Not that he felt Gia was that type of shallow, but he didn't want to take any chances. He had to know for sure.

Ben tried on each article of clothing Matt had hand-selected and decided to purchase all except a few items that were a little *too* snug. "Uh, I took almost your whole pile," Ben said.

"Oh, no worries, man. I wasn't going to buy anything anyway. I just needed to get away from the girl talk. This unexpected meeting worked out well for me. If I came home with all, or any, of those clothes, Carla would have made me crash on the couch tonight!" Matt rolled his eyes. "Apparently, we're on a budget—but really, only me."

"Hey, speaking of girl talk... Has Gia, you know, said anything about me? About us?"

"Nope," Matt said, pinching his fingers together as if holding a zipper and sliding them across his mouth in the my-lips-are-sealed motion. "That would violate the husband/wife privacy act —which extends to the wife's best friends and next-door neighbors."

Ben let out a chuckle. "I understand. I won't pry. I'm just going to have to let this thing play out, I guess. Life is weird, you know? We don't always make the best decisions, or maybe things are just meant to work out how they work out. Everything happens for a reason and all that. I don't know," Ben said, lost in thought momentarily.

"I feel you, bro, but snap out of it. You've got a date tomorrow morning. Go home, pick an outfit, have a drink, get plenty of sleep, and crush it tomorrow! You got this!"

"You sound like a coach. It's a date, not a homecoming game."

Matt shrugged. "Old habits. I was always a jock, remember?"

"I do. The more things change, the more they stay the same!"

"Indeed, they do. Now, let's get outta here." Matt carried half the clothes Ben planned to purchase while Ben took the remainder to the cashier. "Can't wait to hear the damage," Matt said as the cashier started scanning the purchases, the number on the touchscreen in front of them rapidly rising into the multi-hundreds.

"Dude, is this okay?" Matt asked, looking concerned as the total increased.

"No problem," Ben indicated. "It's been a long time since I've gone shopping. I'm overdue. This is over a decade's worth of shopping expenditure here—just happen to be doing it all at once." Matt seemed to think it was an acceptable excuse. After all, the man had been living in the sticks for years and years—he deserved some fresh new clothes. Who was he to judge?

"You got cologne?" Matt asked.

"That's the one thing I *do* have. I'm good."

Throughout his travels, Ben made it a habit to stick to the same cologne he had used since high school. He guessed a woman would call it their 'signature scent,' but to him, the smell anchored him to the past. *La Vie* was the cologne Ben had worn throughout his time with Gia—and before and after—and he saw no reason to change it up now. He was hoping it would be something she fondly remembered.

"Alright then, seems like you don't need me anymore," Matt said. "I guess it's time for me to go home and see what those crazy broads are up to. Here, put my number in your phone. If things work out with you and Gia, maybe we can all hang out some-time." Matt handed Ben a piece of paper with his number jotted, turned, gave a quick wave, and left the store.

Ben smiled. He didn't have many friends in the United States at that point, and he couldn't deny the idea of having another guy to pass the time with regularly was a pleasant one. Ben didn't want to jinx anything, but he couldn't help feeling like maybe things were lining up positively for him. *Maybe everything does happen for a reason,* he thought as he handed his credit card to the cashier, signed the receipt, and then walked back to his car.

When he reached it, he saw her—Jen. She leaned against his car, scrolling through her phone, engrossed in what she was read-ing, as if she'd been waiting for him for a long time.

"Jen, you can't keep showing up like this. You can't keep texting me. I've told you that I'm not interested." Jen looked up from her phone, surprised to see Ben standing there.

"Oh, Benji. I didn't see you there. Why don't we go for a cruise in your sweet ride? Maybe I'll let you teach me how to drive stick shift," Jen purred, tracing her finger down Ben's arm as he tried to gain access to his car.

"Jen. No. Please just stop. This is the last time I'm going to ask nicely. Don't show up at the restaurant, the café, or anywhere else you may think I'll be—or somehow know I'll be. This ends now. Don't make me take the next step."

"Oh, poo, Benji. You're no fun, are you?" Jen moved her lips into an overexaggerated pout. "I'm just looking for a good time. I'll make a deal with you. I'll leave you alone if you give me a little something—you know, for my troubles."

"Are you trying to bribe me?" Ben stared at Jen, shocked at her nerve.

"Consider it a parting gift."

"Not gonna happen. Now move away from my vehicle—or I go get the fine, upstanding police officer I happen to know is standing at the corner of West End and Main Street, and we can explain this little situation."

Jen scoffed, but took a step away from the car, accepting defeat. Ben climbed into his vehicle, turned the engine, and drove off. *I really hope that's the last I see of her.*

Coffee and Car Rides

GIA

Chapter 32

AFTER RETURNING HOME with the perfect dress for her date, handling a few garden chores, and cooking dinner, Gia decided it would be a "take it easy" evening. The children, for the most part, cooperated with their routines. Homework went well, as did bathing, dinner, and bedtime. Gia was grateful for the relatively calm night, knowing it wasn't always that way with the kids. She was nervous about her plans with Ben the next day and felt like a night of tea, reading, and an early bedtime was just what she needed.

As soon as the kids were in bed, Gia threw on her most comfortable sleep pants and a tank top and grabbed the book she'd been trying to finish—a non-fiction gardening guide she'd hoped would take her vertical gardening to the next level—and brewed a cup of strong mint-chamomile tea with dried herbs from her garden. She carried the book and tea upstairs to her bedroom and set them on the nightstand while she climbed into her bed and pulled the covers to her chest. *This is the perfect way to spend the evening,* she thought.

No sooner than the sentiment crossed her mind did her phone buzz softly beside her. Against her better judgment, having decided to avoid the device for the night, she picked it up and glanced at the screen. *Ben. I bet he's canceling.* Gia rolled her eyes. *Men!* Having no choice but to read the message, she clicked it open.

Hey Gia. I'm excited for tomorrow. I hope you are, too. Sleep well, sweet dreams!

"Aww," Gia said aloud. "That was actually really sweet." She smiled, letting a wave of excitement rush over her. She *was* excited, even though everything in her being told her not to let herself get too involved, not to give him that power over her again. She wouldn't get all caught up again! But, despite that commitment, she couldn't ignore that she was genuinely looking forward to the date. *Be cool,* she told herself.

Ben, I'm looking forward to it as well. I haven't been to the botanical garden in years. Goodnight. See you in the morning.

Gia took a deep breath. She picked up her tea and took a sip, letting the brew calm her nerves and relax her senses. She yawned, glanced at her book, then changed her mind about her evening. No book, just sleep. She knew she needed an early bedtime and a good night's sleep. Plus, it gave her less time to worry about what-ifs and could-be's. As she lay in bed, pulling her covers close, Gia couldn't keep a smile from forming across her lips as she considered the next day, wondering what it would bring.

Ben

Ben sat on the couch, trying to focus on the TV while casually sipping a craft beer to calm his nerves. His anxiety over how the next day would go was sky-high. He closed his eyes, threw his neck backward, and groaned. "Ugh, why am I making such a big deal out of this?" he muttered aloud. *Because, bonehead,* he thought, *it IS a big deal. It's why you came back.*

Ben picked his phone up from the coffee table and opened his messaging app, clicking into his trail of texts with Gia. After several attempts at drafting a message that sounded enthused but not overenthusiastic, he finally settled on a quick note indicating he was excited and wishing her a good night of sleep—nothing crazy. Her response came quickly. It was brief, but she also seemed to be looking forward to the day. Ben made one last attempt to focus on the TV show he'd put on before giving up, clicking it off, and heading to bed for the night. *The early bird gets the worm and all that,* he thought.

When he woke up the following day, he felt a combination of nerves and excitement. He sped through his morning routine, giving himself time for a little extra self-care—a long shower, fresh shave, aftershave, a few dabs of cologne, and a bit more hair styling than he would ordinarily include. He walked to his room and opened his closet, now overflowing with new clothing thanks to Matt's makeover. He pulled out the outfit he and Matt had decided was best for the date and dressed.

Matt stepped in front of the closet doors, which also served as a full-length mirror. "Not bad," he said. "Not bad at all!" He turned around for a full view. The dark blue denim of his new jeans flattered his behind more than anything he'd worn recently, and his button-down shirt was snug enough to highlight the broadness of his chest and shoulders without making him look like a muscle-bound gym rat. Overall, he was satisfied with his appearance. He chuckled. *Imagine if I worked out regularly,* Ben pondered as he walked downstairs.

As Ben left his house, he stared at his car for a few moments. *That... That is going to be difficult to explain,* he thought. There was no denying it was an expensive vehicle—a *very* expensive vehicle. He was aiming for a reliance on omission over lies when it came to Gia, so he didn't want to make up a story explaining his car's existence. He'd have to worry about that later. Maybe Gia wouldn't feel comfortable asking at all, and how he procured such a car could just go unsaid for the time being.

Ben left home with enough time to stop for a cup of coffee for himself and Gia on the way to her house. He pulled into a space in front of *Cold Brew.* As he walked toward the entrance, a woman exited the café holding two coffees. He squinted into the sun to get a better look. She wore a floral dress that hugged her curves in all the right places, and her wavy brunette hair was pinned half up to keep it off her face. She was breathtaking. It took him a few moments to realize that it was Gia!

Once he put two and two together, Ben realized she'd also stopped to get them coffee before the drive to the botanical garden. He let out a chuckle, causing Gia to look in his direction. When he caught her eye, a sparkle dancing in his own, he half-yelled, "Fancy meeting you here! I guess great minds think alike."

Gia stared at Ben momentarily, taking in his manly physique and polished look, then started laughing. She had to place her hand over her mouth to stop long enough to speak. "You look great," she finally managed, then glanced down at the two coffees she held. She tilted her head to look up at Ben, holding one out toward him. "Coffee?" she asked, grinning.

"Always," he said, reaching for the travel cup. "Do you need to go home for anything, or should we just start this excursion a bit earlier than planned and leave from here?"

Gia lifted her eyes to the sky, lost in thought, then glanced down into the purse that hung off her shoulder—keys, phone, wallet, and coffee in hand. "I don't think I need to go home for anything."

"Alright, well, you saved me a trip inside! Shall we go?" Ben gestured toward the parking space where his car sat in front of *Cold Brew.*

"Ha ha, very funny," Gia said, rolling her eyes as Ben gestured to the flashy, costly car. Ben didn't laugh in response or pretend to be offended. Instead, he reached into his pocket to unlock the doors and started the engine from the remote. Gia's jaw dropped.

"Borrowed?" she asked.

"Not exactly."

"Rented?"

Ben chuckled. "Nope."

"Yours?" Gia asked, unable to mask the surprise written across her face.

"Mine," Ben confirmed as he walked to the passenger side and opened the door for Gia. He was glad the conversation seemed to end there, as he had decided not to make an excuse for the over-the-top car. Maybe *I should have just rented a cheap car,* Ben thought as he got into the driver's seat and entered the address to the botanical garden into the high-tech GPS.

"Not bad," Ben started. "About forty minutes. Given the earlier-than-expected departure, we may hit some rush hour traffic, but that gives us time to talk." Gia seemed to stiffen uncomfortably at the mention of talking. "Relax. It doesn't have to be *serious* talk. We're on a date, remember? We'll get to know each other—the grownup versions of each other. The new and improved versions, perhaps?"

Gia's expression softened, and the tension left her shoulders as Ben clarified his intent when he said 'talking.' The last thing she wanted to discuss while cooped up in a car with Ben—and with no easy escape route—was their past, or Aiden, for that matter. "I don't know about improved," Gia said, a smile forming. "I feel old as dirt lately!"

"But still as beautiful as ever," Ben said, laying it on thick. "Anyway, we all know how much you enjoy playing in the dirt!"

"I mean, that's true enough."

"You dirty hoe, you," Ben jokingly referencing the profile name Carla had so kindly provided her on *Only Gardeners.* Gia blushed and placed her head in her hands, groaning.

"Oh, hush! That was *all* Carla's doing!"

"Right, sure, uh huh!" Ben said sarcastically. "Hey, who am I to judge? I mean, if you wanna be a dirty garden tool, you do you!" He shrugged exaggeratedly, a wide grin forming across his face as he teased his former flame about her dating profile.

"I'll stick to my garden hose... and hoes! Whatever gets the job done."

"Fair enough. So, speaking of dating profiles, have you had a lot of luck on *Only Gardeners?*" Ben asked, prying for at least some information on where she was in her dating life before they had reconnected.

"I—no. It wasn't even *my* profile. I'd given up dating entirely. It was too messy at this age. Everything was complicated. Everyone had baggage. Carla made the profile, and I think—God, I hope—she only talked to you from it... I have no idea."

"So, I was talking to Carla the whole time?"

"At first, yes."

"Ah... it's safe to assume she knows the truth about Aiden now?"

"Matt and Carla both do. Only since all of this happened."

"I'm sorry they found out this way. I honestly didn't know it wasn't you."

"It's okay. It's not your fault. And, anyway, it was only a matter of time before we had to deal with this situation. Aiden should have been told a long time ago. Maybe now is just... the right time."

Ben couldn't help but wonder if Gia's words were true—and what they might mean for the two of them, if anything at all.

"Hey," Gia started. "I thought we weren't going to talk about this today!"

At first, Ben worried that Gia was annoyed that the subject had shifted to something so serious, but one look at her face told him she was only teasing. Still, it was very much time to change the subject.

The Botanical Garden

GIA

"So, tell me about Brazil. Pretend all the stuff that happened between us didn't exist. Just tell me about your life as if you were telling your stories to someone brand new, someone you've never met before," Gia suggested, curious about Ben's life over the past decade—a life focused around a dream she, too, had hoped to follow.

"Well, it wasn't just Brazil. The truth is, I was all over the place for quite a while—Australia, Africa, other countries in South America. I can't even name all the countries and different regions I've been to off the top of my head. Of course, some are more memorable than others, but the fact is, it all started to feel like a blur. My work allowed me to meet some amazing people, and I learned lessons I would never have otherwise learned, but after a while, when the novelty wore off, it still felt empty. That's when I knew it was time to go home."

"Home to... here?"

"Home to here, yes. But then, when I found out you were divorced, home to... well, you... became more the goal," Ben admitted, taking a deep breath as he realized the change of subject to something lighter had taken an unexpected detour. Nevertheless, he continued. "You're the only person who ever *felt* like home to me, Gia."

Gia's eyes glazed over as she fought back tears of emotion over the impact of his words—words she would have begged him to say years ago. But that was before he left her behind to have a baby alone while he headed off on his personal adventures. "You felt like home to me, too, Ben. Until you didn't. Because you left. I had to hate you to get over you. At the time, it was the only way. Eventually, the hate faded into more of a bitter understanding. We were both young. It was scary. It was terrifying for me, too. But, still... you just left. It's hard to just forget that."

"You're right. We were young. I was selfish and stupid at the time. I couldn't fathom pausing my dreams for anything. I couldn't handle the idea of creating new dreams, or worse, of being trapped here in this town forever."

"So, instead, I got trapped here." Gia glanced at Ben, her hands tightly knit in her lap, thumbs pressed against each other, tapping nervously.

"Do you still feel trapped?"

"No. I love it here now. I have my children, home, garden, and friends. I left the high school Gia behind long ago and started over in the same place with a new life. Then, when I divorced, I did it all over again—and now I couldn't imagine leaving everything I've built. This place is my strength."

"I don't want to leave either. Not anymore. I've been gone long enough..." Ben's voice grew softer and more timid as he added, "But do you ever feel like anything is missing?"

He reached his hand across the center of the vehicle, stretching his fingers out to intertwine them with Gia's. She tensed her shoulders and pressed her lips together, afraid—but intrigued—by where all this was leading. In the interest of finding out, she let Ben hold her hand.

"Sometimes, when it's quiet after the kids have gone with their dad or are at school, when the garden work is finished, and I have nothing pressing to do for work or any other distractions, of course, I get lonely."

"Do you ever think of me?"

"I've tried to avoid it for many years—but lately, you've given me no choice," Gia said, a small smile forming at the edges of her lips.

Grateful to stop the conversation before it could potentially take a turn that could destroy their date, Ben pulled his hand gently away and raised his arm, pointing ahead of them. Gia glanced up and out the window, wishing her hand was still in his momentarily. "We're here!" she exclaimed, taking in the massive welcome sign with "*Botanical Garden*" printed on it, surrounded by decorative floral art. Beneath a banner read "*THIS MONTH: Rare Plant Show!*" Gia felt giddy. She could barely contain her excitement.

"Indeed, we are. Perfect timing." Ben chuckled. "Saved by the garden, I guess." He pulled off the road, driving up the long driveway leading to the garden's parking area, then quickly finding a space, given their early arrival.

"You ready?" Ben asked.

"Ready as I'll ever be," Gia said with a grin.

"Alright, let's do this!"

Ben exited the vehicle, walking around to Gia's side as she gathered her belongings, then pulled the door open and offered his hand to help her out. Together, they walked down the wooded paths leading to the main garden entrance, still holding hands. The garden itself hadn't even started, and already Gia felt her senses getting lost in the magic of nature and botany—the sights and smells of the outdoors. They knew the way by heart. She and Ben had visited this place often, but she never returned after he left. It reminded her of the past—a past she'd worked hard to forget or at least push as far as possible from her mind. When she accepted the date, she figured that if Ben was back, the past was already standing at her feet, staring at her square in the eyes, so what the hell? Why not?

"Remember the *Rainforest Rarities* plant show?" Ben asked, bringing Gia's thoughts back to the present.

"How could I forget it? We practically lived here that month!" Gia said, feeling a slight 'butterflies' sensation dancing in her heart as she remembered the dream-like time they had spent together before she learned about Aiden. She tried to push the feelings away.

"We did. It was pretty amazing." Ben squeezed her hand gently, and despite her concern over the rapidly growing attachment she felt pulling at her, Gia returned the squeeze. It felt weird to be back in this garden with Ben, with their lives under such different circumstances, but she couldn't deny that she was enjoying it.

Gia and Ben finally arrived at the main gate and purchased two tickets to the garden and the extra rare plant show add-ons. When Gia offered to pay for half, Ben immediately turned the offer down. "No, no. You should know me well enough to realize I don't want any of that woman power stuff on dates. I respect you without it, I promise. Now, let me be a gentleman. My treat." He handed his card to the woman behind the gate, and she swiped it.

As Ben accepted it back and put it in his wallet, Gia couldn't help but notice the black "VIP-status" credit card. *Is there something I don't know about him?* She thought back to his fancy car and dinner at *Charmed to Table*. He certainly didn't seem to be struggling, but none of that mattered to her, anyway. She'd learned to make it on her own, and a man with money was equal to a man without in her eyes—the only thing that mattered was love and, possibly even more important, trust. Unfortunately, trust was still seriously lacking with Ben based on their past.

Once inside the botanical garden, Gia and Ben were mesmerized by the myriad of colors and fragrances that overtook their senses, blurring the lines between art and nature. They walked silently through the garden as if the trove of plant life and bright blooms, perfect pops of color amidst the verdant greenery, had stolen their words. It was an impeccably curated homage to the natural world and the wonder of its flora. Some paths gave off a more natural, local woodland vibe, highlighting native species in their full glory, while others were carefully manicured as gardens from exotic landscapes around the world—including stunning rose, orchid, Japanese and British Gardens. Greenhouses throughout the grounds housed the tropical plants in their perfect growing environment, allowing them to thrive.

By the time they reached the structure that housed special events, including the rare plant show, Gia and Ben felt deeply content. The mix of earthy and fragrant floral aromas had left them reeling, feeling dizzy and almost drunk with their shared passion for the garden's beauty.

"I forgot how much I loved it here," Gia said, smiling happily.

Without time for a second thought about whether it was the right or wrong move at that moment, Ben released one of Gia's hands and placed his fingers beneath her chin, lifting it until she looked him in the eyes. "Gia... I will never forget how much I loved you. How much I still love you. How much I will *always* love you."

Ben's words took Gia by surprise. They certainly hadn't followed the rule of sticking to the present during the date, but some things, she guessed, just had to be said.

"Ben, I—"

Before she could finish her sentence, Ben wrapped his free arm around her waist and pulled her in, brushing his lips against hers quickly, then moving her head downward, resting it against his chest with her body tightly held in his embrace. Stunned, Gia thought about pulling away, but everything to her core told her to stay—to just exist in the moment for once.

After a brief pause, Ben leaned slightly downward and whispered against Gia's ear, "I'm sorry, Gia. I'm so sorry for everything. Please forgive me. I promise I'll make it all up to you. Everything. Whether we are together or not, I'll make it up to you."

Moving Slowly

BEN

Chapter 34

FUCK, Ben thought. He hadn't meant to say those words aloud. He hadn't meant to say *anything*; it just slipped out. *Oh well. I just hope I didn't scare her away or lose any progress.* Ben had meant to move slowly with Gia, not allowing his emotions to get the best of him or allow words that couldn't be taken back to escape. He knew Gia was still skittish, given their past, and he was trying to keep his cool despite the emotions boiling to the surface of his heart, growing stronger each time he saw her.

Ben expected Gia to pull away from his embrace, to run again—but she didn't. Instead, she remained with her head pressed against his chest as it rose and fell. They stayed like that for several minutes. Time remained frozen for both as they stood in a close embrace after so long apart. Finally, Gia slowly pulled her head away from Ben's chest and raised her eyes to look into his.

"You can meet Aiden after school today if you'd like," she said. "As my friend."

Ben grinned down at Gia. Tears threatened to invade from the corners of his eyes. He was overtaken with emotion over the opportunity to meet his son—and knowing that Gia felt his intentions were pure enough to at least allow him to play some small role in Aiden's life.

He tried to resist the overpowering desire to kiss Gia again, but it was futile. Ben placed a hand on each of Gia's cheeks and leaned down slightly, gazing into her eyes before pulling her face toward his in a swift motion. He could feel the warmth of her breath against his skin, and for a few seconds, yearning hung heavy in the air like a thick fog. When their lips finally met, it was soft and gentle, like a whisper between lovers. The kiss deepened as Gia slid her tongue through Ben's slightly opened lips, the intensity growing like a spark into a flame.

As their tongues danced to a symphony playing only in their minds, Gia placed a hand against Ben's head, pushing his face harder against her own, then shifted it to the back of his neck. She didn't want the moment to end. She couldn't let go. As their hands wandered across each other's backs, necks, and shoulders, they forgot where they were. The world outside ceased to exist as they held each other again, overcome by the once-familiar feelings lost over time.

Finally, Gia broke the kiss and began to pull away, looking around to be sure they were still alone in that part of the garden. Ben could easily sense that Gia's fear had taken over.

"Ben, I—"

"You don't have to say anything," Ben interrupted. "We don't have to say or do anything right now. Let's enjoy the rest of our date. We just got the end-of-date kiss out of the way a little early, that's all." He gave Gia a friendly squeeze on the shoulder, trying to return to casual interactions. "Let's see the plants. We can talk about... this... later."

Ben tried to make light of the powerful emotions still lingering in the air as he released Gia from his embrace. He reached out to hold her hand, hoping she wouldn't stop him. He could tell she was trying to hold back and avoid getting attached, and he needed to respect that. It was time to slow things down.

Ben led Gia toward the door to the exhibit space, a massive circular greenhouse structure that housed the botanical garden's major plant shows and seasonal exhibits. He released Gia's hand to pull the door open and hold it, gesturing for her to enter ahead of him. Once inside, he placed his arm around her back, hoping it wasn't "too much" under the circumstances.

The massive, all-glass room was bathed in light. The air inside was humid and warm—almost tropical. Ben took in Gia's facial expressions while she walked through the exhibit space, mouth slightly ajar as she read the plaques that provided information on each plant, including native region, potential medicinal, culinary, and other uses, required growing conditions, specific needs, and so on. Most of the plants in the exhibit were challenging to grow without a particular microclimate; therefore, many were kept within their own temperature and moisture-controlled terrariums. As Gia and Ben read the information on each plant, they couldn't help but notice that some combination of habitat destruction, illegal collection, and other human-centered activities also threatened most of them.

"Wow!" Ben said suddenly, unable to hide the excitement in his voice. "I've actually seen these in the wild!" Ben pointed to a leafless, ethereal-looking plant. Delicate white flowers with thin, threadlike petals graced the apex of the stem as it climbed and wound around a host tree.

"Really? They're beautiful! What are they?" Gia asked, peering into the exhibit.

"Ghost orchids!" Ben said with enthusiasm. "They smell incredible, especially at night. Sweet and romantic. The nighttime pollinators *love* them. When I was in Cuba, they grew in one tiny, forested area of a property. We had to avoid building anything nearby that could alter the growing conditions and keep the resort guests out to avoid risking what little habitat they had left. We made sure that—"

"Resort guests? What were you doing in Cuba, exactly? Was it with World Corps?" Gia interrupted before Ben could finish his sentence, triggering the realization that his eco-tourism consulting had been one of his strategic omissions—or, maybe, it just hadn't come up. Either way, he had told Gia he'd done a great deal of traveling but certainly hadn't given her the whole story.

"Well, not exactly. I only stayed with World Corps part of the time I was away. A significant amount of my time abroad involved using the skills I acquired while volunteering with them to help other companies establish more environmentally friendly, sustainable resorts in rainforest areas."

"Oh, so, like eco-tourism?" Gia questioned.

"Exactly. I became an eco-tourism consultant, hence the traveling. I started my own company. It was quite successful."

"That's fascinating!"

"It was definitely an experience. It was..." Ben trailed off, then paused, pondering whether he should share any further details about just *how* successful the company was. Finally, he decided if he couldn't be honest now, there was no point in continuing to court Gia. He knew he needed to build her trust—and he could tell she wasn't after his money at this point, so... why not? "It was quite lucrative," he added.

"Lucrative? How lucrative?" Gia asked, narrowing her eyes.

Ben's eyebrows raised and his shoulders naturally moved into a shrug, but he remained silent.

"The car?" Gia squinted at Ben. "*That* lucrative?"

Ben nodded, a chuckle escaping. "That lucrative."

"Oh... I... Oh. Um, wow. Congratulations, I guess!" Gia stumbled to get the sentence out, unsure how to take the unexpected news of Ben's wealth.

"I didn't tell you because, well, I don't actually know, honestly. I guess I just wasn't sure how. And I didn't know if it would make you think of me differently. I didn't want it to. I'm still the same guy I always was—nothing has changed. Well, no, I mean, I've changed, of course—but in good ways. I've grown up." It was Ben's turn to trip over his words as he realized the whole point of returning home and seeking out Gia was to prove to her that he *had* changed. He needed her to know he was a far cry from the boy who ran away from his problems many years ago.

"There are some other things you should probably know sooner rather than later, but let's take this one step at a time." Ben couldn't help but wonder if he should share that his career path had taken another recent transition into being a restaurant and café owner or hold off based on his original intentions. Ultimately, he decided to hang onto that piece of information.

He had a plan for it.

"Other things like what?" Gia asked, wondering what else he could possibly have up his sleeve.

"Oh, don't worry about it. You'll see. It's nothing bad. I promise. No more about me now, though. Please, back to the plants! Can we just get back to the plants?" Ben pleaded, a teasing grin forming across his features. Gia chuckled, unsure how to process the situation she now found herself in.

"Okay, okay! Back to the plants. Now, then, tell me more about ghost orchids," Gia said as she peered, once again, at the breathtaking rare flowers.

"They're called ghost orchids because, well, because they look ghostly," Ben said, realizing how dumb it sounded only after the words had left his mouth.

Gia couldn't control the laugh that escaped her mouth. "Well, thank you, Captain Obvious. Good thing I have you as my guide, Mr. I've-Seen-Them-in-the-Wild-in-Cuba. Where would I be without your botany expertise?"

They both started laughing as they walked toward the next plant exhibit, Ben's arm still wrapped around Gia's waist.

Passion, Plans, and Proposals

GIA

Chapter 35

THE THOUGHTS in Gia's head had been swirling ever since the incredible kiss she'd shared with Ben. She could barely focus on the extraordinary plants before her! The distraction of trying to re-live the kiss in her mind overpowered her ability to think clearly. It was as if a fire that had burned out long ago had been re-ignited, shaking her deep down to her very core and sending shockwaves through her entire body. Every part of her, both physical and emotional, wanted to kiss Ben again and again—and again. At the same time, she felt torn. She couldn't help but think of the complications.

The baggage. There was baggage from the past and the present, and it would exist well into the future. *Could we ever get past all that?* Gia wondered. *Do I have a life he would ever even be interested in having? The house, the kids, it's chaos. But... if not, then why is he here with me?*

Gia's mind churned out thought after thought, but finally, she managed to calm the flow of questions to a dull roar, enjoying the present moment and company. As Gia and Ben laughed over ghost orchids, everything felt right. She felt comfortable. The only way she could verbalize the feeling that had come over her was the same way Ben had described it—home. She felt at home with Ben. Maybe it was because he knew her past—the good and the bad. She hid so many parts of herself from other people, but Ben knew the real Gia from their time as friends, then more. Still, Gia couldn't help but acknowledge that *he* was the reason she'd been so guarded with all of the others who came after.

Together, they walked the rare plant exhibit space. Ben's arm had remained wrapped around Gia's waist since their kiss, and Gia wasn't about to move it. She could no longer deny that she wanted to feel the rest of him wrapped around her as well, limbs tangling in passion. *Gia, control yourself.* Despite many attempts to push them from her mind, the thoughts remained the backdrop to the morning excursion.

By the time they'd wandered the large, open area several times over, reading the plant plaques and taking mental notes about which interested them most, their uses, and so on, Gia and Ben's flirting had reached an all-time high. They made jokes about the aphrodisiac flora, laughing and blushing. When they reached the exit to the large, glass building, Ben pushed the door open and held it for Gia.

"So, what now?" Ben asked.

"Hmm," Gia said, thinking. "What time is it?"

Ben glanced at his watch. "Around lunchtime. When do you need to be home?"

"Well, the kids will be home at around four, but Carla is on-call to get them off the bus. I made sure to have a backup in case we hit traffic or something and I couldn't get home in time. If I'm a little late, it's okay. I'll just have to text Carla."

"Always the planner." Ben grinned. "Let's head back. If you want, we can go to lunch at *Charmed to Table*. I want to tell you a few things, and I think that's the best place to do it. We won't be long, and it's close to home."

"Okay, fine," Gia began, more than pleased to check out the *Charmed to Table* lunch menu, "but we are *not* ordering the entire dessert menu this time! I'll never fit into my pants with you around!"

"Pants are overrated, anyway," Ben said with a wink.

"That may be so, but I'd like to fit into mine just the same. If they're coming off, I want to have a say!" Gia chuckled, trying to avoid imagining Ben pantsless, afraid of the effect it'd have on her ability to maintain her composure. "I don't have an endless clothing budget, y'know?"

Ben

Ben couldn't help but wince thinking about the absurd amount of money he had just spent on clothes for himself the day before. It was a needed expenditure and far from a financial burden under his circumstances, but still, with the exception of his car, it wasn't like him to spend money on himself. *Oh well, at least I look good,* he thought to himself. *More importantly, Gia seems to think so.*

Ben had noticed Gia's eyes wandering across his arms, chest, shoulders, and even downward several times throughout their date. It's not like he could fault her for it. He couldn't help himself, either. He had been eyeing her up and down as discreetly as possible all morning, trying to keep his eyes from getting stuck on anything that could get him in trouble. To Ben, Gia was the perfectly put-together woman—stunning natural beauty, a breathtakingly curvy figure, and a smile that could knock him off his feet every time. Many years had passed since they'd been together last, but Ben thought she looked even better now than when they were young. Her body had filled out in all the right places, and on a few different occasions over the course of the date, he had to force himself to look the other way to keep his composure in her presence.

Having his arm around her waist was torture enough, but that kiss nearly took him past the point of no return. Ben knew it sounded cheesy, but he saw stars. He had to pull away, breaking from the kiss in the midst of its perfection, not only because he didn't want to scare Gia away but because he needed to get himself under control. He wanted nothing more than to hold her in his arms, to wrap himself around her and feel her pressed against his chest, to feel her body and take in all of its softness and curves, but the timing wasn't right. Not yet, anyway.

There were still things to discuss and bring to light—big plans. Ben could only hope Gia would be on board with them because he needed her—for himself *and* his business. Even if Gia wasn't willing to give their relationship another try, he hoped she'd take him up on the business side of things. If everything went according to plan, their lunch at *Charmed to Table* would be the perfect time for the revelation, and he hoped Gia would accept his proposal—business proposal, that was. *Let's not get ahead of ourselves here.*

Sharing with Gia that he owned *Charmed to Table*—and *Cold Brew*—wasn't a ploy to "get her back" or show off his financial gains abroad. Over a brief period, the café and restaurant had become his pride and joy—each for different reasons. Ben knew he needed Gia's plant and garden knowledge, creative farm-to-table recipes, marketing ingenuity, and culinary expertise to bring *Charmed to Table* to the next level. It could be so much more than just a restaurant, and he knew that, together, they could perfect it.

He needed a partner.

Not just any partner, though. He needed someone competent and passionate enough to take the reins of all aspects of the restaurant while he was tied up with logistics for *Cold Brew.* The global networking involved in *Cold Brew's* operations was a full-time job in itself. He needed Gia. His "thing" had always been coffee, whereas he felt *Charmed to Table* was the perfect creative outlet for Gia—and he trusted her, something he only hoped he could earn back in return over time.

Ben's primary concern was that Gia would see this as a charity offering or nothing more than him trying to make up for his past transgressions. He supposed, somehow, it was—but the truth was that she was the best person for the role. He didn't need financial backing; he needed someone who would be as committed to the restaurant as he was, someone who wanted it to succeed. Their first visit to *Charmed to Table*, however unplanned, had proved her interest.

As Ben and Gia walked to the garden exit, Ben stopped in front of a photo booth near the season ticket sales station. "Come on, Gia. We have to! For old time's sake, if nothing else." Ben ducked into the booth, holding his hand out to Gia from behind the curtain. They had taken a photo at that booth practically every time they'd gone to the garden. The booth had been updated to a much more modern model over time, but the overall concept was still the same.

"Tradition is tradition," Gia agreed, stepping into the booth and sitting on the bench beside Ben. The machine of their youth took only cash, whereas this one accepted several different forms of payment. Ben swiped his credit card through the machine, and the screen before them lit up with a variety of photo and filter options to choose from. The process was much more interactive than it once was and included a variety of prop stickers and more to add to the photos.

Gia and Ben cackled as they tried several different poses with each other, then digitally selected different hats, glasses, backgrounds, and phrases to include on the prints. Ultimately, they settled on a series of photos with Gia grinning, wearing a wide-brimmed garden hat and Ben with a pair of overalls and a sprig of straw between his lips amidst a field of sunflowers in the background. The photo read "Together Again!"

As they awaited the final product to print, Gia turned to Ben. "Do you still have them?" Gia asked.

"Of course. Do you?" Ben said, knowing she was referring to his copies of their previous garden photos.

"Always," Gia said.

Ben ran a finger down her cheek and across her lips, sending tingles down her spine. Their eyes met, and Ben's hand shifted to the back of Gia's head, moving his face toward hers.

"Gia, I can't not kiss you. I just want to keep kissing you," he whispered, their lips nearly touching.

"Then do it," Gia murmured between pursed lips, awaiting his. The request was immediately granted as Ben's lips pressed against hers. More fireworks. The kiss was passionate, deep, and long. Their hands wandered, shielded from the public by the curtain and less inhibited this time, gripping backs, necks, and faces, lost in each other's long-forgotten caresses.

Lost in the moment, they would have continued for the rest of the day had they not been interrupted by the photo machine beeping incessantly to announce that their prints were ready. As Gia reached down to grab the sheets, Ben pulled the curtain aside momentarily and glanced out, seeing a family awaiting their turn in the booth. He closed the curtain, rolling his eyes slightly. *No one ever uses this booth, and now there's a line.*

"To be continued?" Ben asked, turning to face Gia.

"I hope so," Gia confessed, raising the photos in front of them so they could share their first look simultaneously. They stared at the picture, then at each other, before erupting into a fit of giggling. Gia in her too-big hat and Ben with his hillbilly overalls were just too much for them to handle. They looked so goofy —yet perfect—together. Gia ripped the print in half, splitting the photos between them to add to their collections, which, apparently, they'd both held onto. Gia and Ben slid out of the booth one after the other and stepped down, nodding to those awaiting their turn, still barely able to hold back their laughter as they headed toward the car.

"Now, we eat," Ben said, opening the car door for Gia before moving around to the driver's side.

"Can't wait!" Gia placed her hand on Ben's leg just above his knee, sending chills through his body. "That was fun," she added.

"It was fun. I missed that."

"Me too."

Private Party

CARLA

Chapter 36

"I'm gonna call her..." Carla reached into her hoodie pocket and pulled out her phone, but as quickly as it appeared, Matt snatched it from her hands. "Hey! I—"

"Don't you dare. For the love of God, leave them alone!" Matt said, slapping his palm against his forehead dramatically. "Can't you let them have one measly date without inserting yourself into it somehow?"

"In my defense, *Matty,* they wouldn't even be *having* a date if it weren't for me helping or—as you refer to it—inserting myself into things." Carla scoffed, grabbing her phone back from Matt. "But, fine. I won't call. She should be back soon, anyway. The kids..." Carla trailed off, just remembering she was "on duty" as a backup to watch the kids if Gia was running late. "Either way, we'll hear from her soon enough!"

"Good. Problem solved. The mystery will unravel soon. So, to be continued. Anyway, I'm hungry. What're we eating?"

"That's what she said," Carla said, her tone suggestive. Matt rolled his eyes, but a grin crept up his mouth.

"You have a dirty mind. Lunch. I'm discussing lunch. Let's try this again... What are we eating for lunch?" Matt walked up behind Carla, tickling her just beneath the ribs and kissing her neck softly.

"Hmm, there's not much here. Do you want to go out? Believe it or not, *Charmed to Table's* menu was pretty enticing. I haven't been able to stop thinking about some of the entrees since we ditched Ben and Gia there."

"Yeah, that actually sounds good. I could use a lunch outing —and we have just about enough time to make it there and back before the bus arrives, just in case we need to get the kids," Matt said, offering a gentle reminder that they were still on-call to keep an eye on Gia's kids.

"Oh, right. I forgot already. What would I do without you? See? This is probably why we don't have kids. I'd lose my sense of maternal responsibility and leave them someplace as soon as I got a little bit hungry."

"You'd be just fine, my love. You'd make a wonderful mother. Okay, let's head out. Time's a'wasting!"

Gia

"Hey, Ben?" Gia asked, tucking a stray hair behind her ear and glancing over at Ben in the driver's seat.

"Mmhmm?" Ben responded, his eyes still on the road.

Gia didn't continue immediately, lost in thought and fiddling with Ben's fancy car radio as they headed toward *Charmed to*

Table for lunch. "Do you think you'll be sticking around here for a while? Any plans to make a rapid escape to another country or...?"

"Well, I have several reasons to stay. I think it's safe to say I have no immediate exit strategy." Ben paused and glanced at Gia as they reached a red light. "Gia, the reality of the situation is I'm ready to stay put somewhere. I spent a long time jumping from place to place, never staying enough time for it to feel like my home. This town is the only place that ever really felt that way. And now, that's really all I want—a sense of stability, comfort, all the things I felt were missing during those adventures. As I said, several things are keeping me here at present."

Gia nodded, trying to hide the smile that was forming against her better judgment.

"Like what?" Gia asked.

"You'll see," Ben said, reaching over to hold Gia's hand as they pulled into the municipal parking lot on Main Street. Given the time of day—the end of the lunch rush—street parking would be a challenge, and it was only a short walk from the lot to the restaurant. He parked the car and squeezed Gia's hand gently before climbing out. As Gia fumbled to gather her belongings, Ben opened the passenger-side door for her.

Together, they walked down Main Street toward the restaurant. It was a beautiful day, and the sun shone high in the sky. It put a bit of extra pep in Gia's mood, making her feel a little giddy —or maybe that was the present company, she wasn't sure.

Upon their arrival at *Charmed to Table*, Ben stepped up to the hostess booth. The hostess, a pretty girl of about twenty, smiled brightly at them. "Ben! Nice to see you. Work or pleasure?" the hostess inquired, causing a confused glance to cross Gia's face.

"Let's just call it lunch with an old friend." Ben chuckled. "Is it okay if we dine in the back section—the one that is typically closed at lunchtime? We have some catching up and a few things to discuss privately."

"Of course. You're the boss," the hostess said, smiling as she grabbed a couple of menus and a beverage list and directed them to follow toward the back of the restaurant. Ben glanced over at Gia, noticing her confusion.

"I'll explain momentarily," he whispered to Gia. "No time like the present and all that." Ben pulled out a chair for Gia and walked to the opposite side of the small, two-person table.

"Do you know her... *Boss*?" Gia asked, emphasizing the word *boss*.

"Who?"

"The hostess."

"I do. It all ties in with something I'm trying to tell you. A few things, in fact."

"Okay, well, you're making me nervous. Stop being cryptic. Can you just spit it out?"

"Let me ask you something first... What do you think of this new branding?" Ben pulled out a pile of papers, folded once, from within the interior of his jacket. It appeared to be a mock-up of a new sign for the front of the restaurant. The sign had a cozy yet elegant look, with sage green plants winding across it, their stems forming the letters of the words *Charmed to Table*.

"It's gorgeous. It's perfect! But why are you involved in the restaurant's branding? Are you working in marketing now that you're back? Is this one of your clients? Oh! That's how you know the hostess. I get it now!"

"Uh, well... not exactly. I kind of... Well, Gia... I kind of own it," Ben said, fidgeting uncomfortably with the revelation. "What do you think about *this* one?"

Ben pulled another mock-up from his pile. At first glance, it was identical, but upon closer examination, Gia noticed a single word had been added in a different font just above *Charmed to Table*. There, clear as day, was her name: *Gia's Charmed to Table*.

"It's beautiful, but I don't understand," Gia began. "Why would you put—"

"I need a partner, Gia. In the restaurant, I mean." Ben stammered, his words tangling before they could even make it out of his mouth. "In other areas as well, but that's a whole different can of worms."

"Oh, Ben... I don't have any—"

"I don't need money, Gia," Ben cut her off. "I'm not looking for an investor or financial partner in any sense of the word. Money, I have; it's time and ability I'm short on. I want your expertise, skills, and passion for all *Charmed to Table* stands for. There is so much possibility here, so much opportunity for growth and to make a difference. I just don't have it in me to make this place all it could be with *Cold Brew* taking up so much of my time."

"... *Cold Brew?*" Gia asked hesitantly. "Why is *Cold Brew* taking up your time?"

Ben froze. He hadn't planned to reveal that bit of information just yet. "Well, I guess the cat's out of the bag, as they say. I... I sort of own that, too."

"Jesus Christ, Ben! Do you own the whole damn town?!"

"No," Ben shrugged, "just those two." He appeared to be some combination of embarrassed and proud.

"So, you own the only decent coffee shop and restaurant in town? Why didn't you tell me sooner?"

"I don't know. I wanted to see how things went. I didn't want you to think of me differently than you used to."

"Ben," Gia started, "I hated you. I don't think it could have gotten any worse for us if you'd told me that."

"I know—and rightfully so—but until I left, you didn't. I guess I just wanted to see how you felt about me as a person rather than, well..." Ben winked at Gia, nodded his head in mock confidence, and added, "as a wildly attractive, extremely successful entrepreneur and businessman."

"Ben, I really don't know what to say," Gia said. "I'm proud of you, though. This is incredible."

"Then say yes. This partnership would be an amazing opportunity for you—and it would be a huge weight off my shoulders to know the restaurant is in your hands when I can't oversee things. It would be, for the most part, yours. Name right on the sign and all!"

"It would be a dream come true, but it's just too much!"

"Come on, Gia. Let me do this for you. I would be lying if I said I didn't have past transgressions to atone for, and maybe this is *partly* about that—but is it so wrong of me to want to try to fix my mistakes? To make up for them in some small way? I can't go back and change the past—but I can ensure you have a stable future for yourself and the kids. Please. You can make this place even greater than it is now—I know you can!"

Gia sighed deeply, considering Ben's offer. "A trial," she finally said.

"Huh?"

"Let's do it as a trial—one month. I'll manage *Charmed to Table*. We'll make decisions together, brainstorm, plan, and see how things go. If you still want me to be your partner at the end of the month, I'm in. It'll be like when we were planning for Brazil."

Ben winced noticeably at the mention of their joint plans for Brazil, clearly wanting to move away from that subject as quickly as possible, given how it had left the two of them.

"Deal," Ben said, reaching across the table for Gia's hand and giving it a firm shake. "Now, let's eat! What're we having?"

"Well, we already ordered all the desserts... How do you feel about taste testing all the apps? If I'm going to help run this place, I need to sample the options!" Gia grinned.

"I'm in. Let's do it. Hang here. I'll go put the order in," Ben said, rising. "I'm kinda a big deal around here, you know." He puffed his chest out as he strutted toward the kitchen but stopped short when he reached the access point to the main dining room.

"Uh... Gia? How do you feel about some company?" Ben asked, one eyebrow raised.

Gia looked at him quizzically. "Huh?"

"Come here." Ben gestured to the main dining room. "Look," he said, grinning. Gia walked over to Ben and glanced out the doorway, her eyes moving in the direction he was pointing.

"Oh! It's Carla and Matt. Are they following us? Do they know—you know—about you—about the restaurant and café?" Gia wondered if they'd come looking for her, knowing Ben owned *Charmed to Table*.

"Nope. I guess they felt they missed out on a good meal the other day when they bailed on us. I mean, we do have a pretty awesome menu. Should we treat them to a full buffet of appetizers in what's currently acting as our 'private party room' to make up for it?"

"Yes!" Gia couldn't hide her excitement at sharing the news of the potential partnership—in the restaurant business—with Carla. "Can we have their waitress get them back here and surprise them?"

"Of course," Ben said, waving one of the waitresses on the floor over and asking her to "reseat" their friends in the back room. They watched as Matt and Carla collected their personal effects with confused expressions as the waitress gathered their menus and led them toward the back room. Gia and Ben returned to their seats, waiting to see the looks on their faces when her friends saw the two of them dining at the private table.

"Surprise!" Gia and Ben yelled in unison, taking Carla and Matt by surprise as they walked into the back dining room.

It's a Celebration!

CARLA

CARLA COULDN'T HIDE her expression of surprise at finding Ben and Gia dining in the back room of *Charmed to Table*. "Uh... hi guys!" she exclaimed, walking toward the table for two. "Private party?"

"Something like that," Gia said. "We *are* celebrating in a sense."

"Oooh, celebrating, huh? Celebrating what exactly?" Carla asked, raising an eyebrow.

"A new partnership," Ben chimed in, reaching over the table and squeezing Gia's hand.

Carla squealed at the sound of the word *partnership*. "I knew you two were going to wind up together!" she blurted out, unable to contain her excitement. "You can thank me later!" She winked at Gia, grinning.

"Not *that* type of partnership," Ben said with a groan. "A professional partnership. Welcome to *Gia's Charmed to Table!*"

"Trial," Gia interjected, "It's only a trial." Noting the confusion written across Carla and Matt's faces, she added, "As it turns out, Ben owns this restaurant."

Matt and Carla exchanged glances before shifting their gazes back to Gia and Ben. "What do you mean he *owns* the restaurant?" Carla asked.

"*Cold Brew,* too." Gia shrugged. "A man of many secrets, it seems."

"Benjamin, bro! You've been holding out on me," Matt said. "All the time we spent together last night—and you left out the most interesting parts! So, uh... Could I get free food and coffee from this stellar new friendship?" Matt elbowed Ben playfully in the ribs.

Unaware of Ben's prior evening with Matt, Gia threw a quizzical look in Ben's direction. "It's a long story," he said as Carla rolled her eyes.

"Do you ever think about anything but food?" she asked, nudging Matt in his ribcage.

"I think we all know the answer to that question... Sometimes I think about sex, too." Matt chuckled, wrapping his arm around Carla's waist. "And how much I love my very beautiful, albeit meddlesome wife. So, Gia will be managing the restaurant, then?"

"We'll see how it goes after a one-month trial partnership. In the restaurant, I mean," Gia said, flustered over the resurfacing of the word "partnership" in connection with her and Ben.

"Among other things, I hope," Carla muttered under her breath, smirking at Gia and Ben, who were still holding hands without either one even realizing it.

Gia jumped to change the subject to avoid further discussion about her and Ben and what they were, weren't, would be, or could be. "Well, your timing is impeccable—even though you're supposed to be home in an hour to collect my offspring at the bus stop. You're off the hook for that, by the way. I'll get home in time. Meanwhile, to celebrate this new development, we are treating you two to a complimentary sampling of the entire appetizer menu. You know, to make up for you losing out on your meal here the other day."

"Drinks, too, of course!" Ben added.

"Oh, hell yeah!" Matt said, eyeing the dishes as a waiter began placing an array of platters on the bar surface behind them. "Those look amazing!"

"Well, they are," Ben began, "but Gia and I are open to any suggestions to make them—or any other dishes—even better. Now, eat up!"

Together, the group walked over to the bar and began loading up their plates with different types of appetizers, including stuffed mushrooms, herb-marinated olives, local meats and cheeses, deviled eggs with fresh herbs, grilled vegetables with lemon juice, crostini with goat cheese and local fruit, and more.

"This all looks amazing," Carla said. "I can't wait to see what else you come up with, Gia. You're such a great gardener *and* cook. I'm sure you have tons of ideas."

"I knew Gia was the perfect woman for the job!" Ben smiled at Gia. "Now, let's get some drink orders in before Gia heads home to get the kids. You guys are welcome to stay back here as long as you like. I'll be sure you're well taken care of—and whatever else you want is on me, of course. Just let the waitress know what you need."

"Wow, this is delicious!" Carla said, chewing a thin slice of toast topped with fresh tomato bruschetta while reading the drink menu. "I think I'll try the jalapeno pineapple margarita. That sounds like it's right up my alley."

"An excellent choice," Ben said. "One of my favorites!"

"Make that two," added Matt.

"Three," Gia grinned, "but just one—then I have to go."

"Well, may as well follow the crowd," Ben said, stepping out to the main dining room, where the larger bar was located, to tell the bartender.

꜀꜀

Gia

As Ben walked out of the back area of the restaurant to give their drink order to the bartender, Gia leaned in to whisper to Matt and Carla, who were still stuffing themselves with the restaurant's entire offering of appetizers.

"You guys... I think... I think I'm falling for him." Gia groaned, putting her head down into her hands. "And I don't want to do that—especially now that his business is involved. Ugh!"

"Gia, for the love of God! This is your second chance with him. Stop worrying so much about all that could go wrong. For once in your life, start thinking about what could go right. He came back from a life of adventure to this boring, small town— potentially to be with you. He's obviously been quite successful, to boot!" Carla said.

"It wasn't to *be with me,*" Gia said. "At least, I don't think it was. It couldn't have been. There's no way."

"Gia, listen... it all lines up. Maybe this started because he wanted to be in Aiden's life, but it sure looks like he is here for more now. He could have found someone else to put into your role in the restaurant, but he wanted you. He didn't have to swipe right on your dating profile, but he did. He didn't have to take you out on a date, but he did. For once, accept that this could be a good thing—a *really* good thing—and just let it play out."

"Shush!" Gia said as Ben made his way back to the table. "He's coming."

"Alright, drink order is in. Jalapeno pineapple margaritas for all within five minutes!" Ben pulled a chair out at the table and sat, realizing his company had become silent on his return. "So, what were we talking about?"

"Nothing," blurted Gia, Carla, and Matt simultaneously. Ben narrowed his eyes and glanced around the table, chuckling.

"Well, that's very convincing, you guys. Okay, okay, I'll leave you to your secrets. I get it. I'm the new guy. Or... the old guy who's now new, or... you know what I mean," Ben said, stumbling over his words. "So, what are the votes for the favorite appetizer so far?"

Carla pointed to her plate and, with her mouth full, mumbled, "Bruschetta, no question."

"No. The mushrooms. The stuffed mushrooms are absolutely incredible," Matt said as he popped one into his mouth.

"I can't choose!" Gia said.

"Well, I'm glad they're all good. And I know Gia will make them even better." Ben squeezed her arm gently in reassurance. As the waitress arrived with their margaritas, he grabbed two off the tray. "Hey, Gia, can I talk to you privately for a second?"

Carla and Matt exchanged glances as Gia rose to follow Ben through a curtain leading to a room used primarily for restaurant storage

The Supply Closet

BEN

Chapter 38

BEN LED Gia away from the table and down the hallway into the restaurant's dry storage room, hoping to get a moment of the privacy he'd hoped to have during their interrupted lunch. He carried their drinks, carefully setting them on one of the lower pantries.

"Gia," he began, taking a deep breath. "I need you to know that I came back here for you. For Aiden, of course. I want to know him. The truth of the matter is that I came back for us. To see if there could ever even be an us again. I know it's complicated. I know we both have a lot of... emotional baggage, for lack of a better word. Our history is dicey, but I want to make it up to you. I'm in a place where I can do that now. I want to be in your life *and* Aiden's—and the others, of course."

Tears began to form in the corners of Gia's eyes, threatening to stream down her face. "Ben, I wanted you to come back for so long. Even after Steve and I got together, I hoped so hard you'd change your mind. But you didn't. You stayed. Now, I just don't know. Everything is harder."

"I tried... it was too late. Maybe it doesn't have to be harder. We are lucky enough to get another chance to at least see how things go. Don't tell me you don't feel the connection between us. I know you do. You can't tell me it isn't still there." Ben reached down and held both of Gia's hands. "It's always been there. You can't deny it."

"You're right. I can't deny it, but like you said, it's complicated. You don't even know my kids—one of whom is your own son."

"So, let's start slow. But let's start somewhere. It's not fair not to try at all. Listen, can I still meet Aiden after school?"

Gia wiped away a tear that had escaped down her cheek, looking Ben in the eyes. "Yes," was all she said, pulling him close and burying her face against his chest. Ben wrapped his arms around her and held tightly, breathing in the sweet smell of lavender from her skin. He brushed a stray strand of hair behind her ear. They stayed in the embrace for several minutes, feeling the comfort of home that only their connection with each other could offer—the home that had been missing for so long.

Finally, Gia lifted her head off Ben's chest and tilted it upward to look into his eyes. "We should try," she whispered. "I do want to try."

Ben gazed at her, placing his hands on either side of her face, cupping it gently, and bent to press his lips against hers first softly, then harder. There was a sense of urgency behind the kiss that hadn't been there the last time. It was as if they were diving headfirst into something neither had the power to stop—a rush of passion that consumed them like wildfire, a desire rooted in nostalgia, lust, apprehension about the future, and a deep longing that burned like embers from a past flame that was never fully extinguished.

Gia's tongue separated Ben's lips, finding its way inside to dance with his. She felt lost in the ecstasy of his embrace, yet somehow found at the same time—as if she'd been aimlessly wandering all this time and only now discovered where she truly belonged. Ben's hands wandered, tracing fingers across Gia's sundress and exposed skin. "I missed you," he murmured as he pushed her back gently against the wall on the far side of the room.

"I—missed—you—too," Gia managed to say, pulling away to speak each rushed word between Ben's kisses. "And I want you."

Ben pulled away slightly, gazing into Gia's eyes with lust, taking in her natural beauty. "Oh my God, Gia. I want you so bad it hurts," Ben said, running the fingers of one hand softly across the top of her chest, then dipping lower, crossing her scoop neck-line. His other hand moved downward, playing with the hem of her dress as he bent to kiss lower, down and across her neck.

Gia tilted her head back, then to the side as Ben moved across her neck with his lips. A small moan escaped her mouth as she ran her fingers through his hair. Over the thin material of Gia's floral dress, he cupped one breast in his hand and squeezed gently, causing her to moan again, this time more deeply. He pinched her nipple through the fabric, then reached behind to unclasp Gia's bra, raising her arms and lifting it and the dress over her head, tossing it aside.

Gia lifted Ben's muscular arms, pulling his shirt off. Her hands wandered over his strong chest, tracing the curvature of his solid pectoral muscles. She kissed him passionately again, holding his face in her hands, then began to move downward, trailing her tongue over his neck, then kissing all across his chest and down his torso. As she bent her knees, she caressed his ass and teased, running her fingers across his abdomen, just under the waistline of his pants.

"Gia, you're driving me crazy," Ben said, breathing heavily.

"Good," she whispered, fiddling with the button of his pants. "That's what I'm—"

She was stopped mid-sentence by a click and squeak—the sound of the door to the storage room opening—and Carla's surprised voice. "Oh my God, I'm sorry. I—I'm so sorry." Carla took a step back, covering her eyes. "Don't you know how to lock a door? What the hell?"

Gia rose quickly, grabbing her dress from where it had landed on a shelving unit and covering her practically naked body as best she could. "I—we—we were talking," Gia stuttered.

"I see that. Talking." Carla rolled her eyes. "Half-naked talking. Listen, I'm the last one to judge. You can get your jollies off however and whenever you want, but I was coming to tell you that you—or I, if you'd like to stay here and... finish—need to leave to get your kids off the bus. Like, now-ish."

"What?" Gia glanced at her watch. "Oh my God! We just got in here. How did the time pass so quickly?"

"It happens," Carla said, smirking. "Trust me."

"Ben, I'm sorry. I have to go. Now," Gia said, her embarrassment over the situation clouded by the urgency of ensuring someone was at the bus stop to pick up the kids. She frantically pulled her dress back on and smoothed it out.

"Can I come?" Ben asked.

"I mean... I already interrupted that, but maybe you guys could try again later." Carla chuckled to herself, clearly pleased with her joke. Ben rolled his eyes, grabbed his shirt, and put it on.

"Gia—can I come with you?" he repeated.

"Yes. But we need to leave right now."

Ben grinned, realizing the implication was that she would allow him to meet the kids. "Let's roll," he said, adjusting his now-tighter pants and the rest of his clothes to appear more presentable.

"Let's take your car. It's closer. We can discuss the details of how we're doing this. It might get complicated. Aiden isn't stupid or a toddler. Carla, can you or Matt drive my car home whenever you leave?"

"You got it!" Carla said, giddy with the knowledge that her meddling had led two former lovers back into each other's arms —and would potentially be reuniting a father with his son.

Ben and Aiden

GIA

GIA AND BEN arrived at her house with time to spare before the bus arrived. During the car ride, they'd discussed what they would tell the children about Ben and who he was. Together, they decided they'd start by introducing Ben as an old friend from high school and, if necessary, detail the new restaurant partnership. They could only hope the questions remained at a bare minimum—especially from Aiden. From there, they'd reveal Ben as Aiden's father when the time was right. They didn't assign a timeline to that part of the plan.

"Steve is going to need to be there, or at least know when it's happening," Gia told Ben. "Aiden hasn't known any father but him for his whole life."

"I get that," said Ben. "I'll do this when and however you want. I'm just grateful you're letting it happen."

Gia and Ben exited the car, which Ben had pulled up to the curb in front of her house.

"Just so you know," Gia started. "My kids are going to flip out when they see this car." She gestured to the flashy vehicle and chuckled. "It's right up Aiden's alley."

"I'll take them for a ride sometime. Hey, actually, maybe we could all go for a ride. Ice cream?"

"Do you own an ice cream shop, too?" Gia smirked.

"Not yet." Ben chuckled. "But not out of the question. Got any in mind? I'm always up to expand my horizons—especially in the realm of ice cream. Fresh, locally sourced dairy ice cream. I mean, it fits, right? And who doesn't like ice cream?"

Gia laughed. "Slow down there, tiger. Aren't you adding me as a partner because you don't have enough time to devote to *Charmed to Table?* One thing at a time."

"I didn't get where I am now with one thing at a time, you know." Ben smiled at Gia. "It was more like... all the things, all at once, until I barely even knew which way was up. And it worked out pretty well so far. Really only missing one thing..."

"What's that?" Gia asked.

"I have a feeling you know exactly what it is." Ben reached out and took Gia's hand.

She blushed, realizing he was referring to her. Before she could respond, she heard the bus moving down the road toward the bus stop just outside Gia's house. She dropped Ben's hand and stepped away. "Saved by the bus," she said. "Now, buckle up. Here we go. You ready?"

"No," muttered Ben. "But... Ready or not, it's time. I want to know my son."

The bus pulled up, and its stop sign swung outward as it came to a stop. The door opened, and three children bounded down the bus steps toward their mother, each going in for a quick hug. "Whoa, mom! Did we get a new car?!" the tallest boy asked, staring with his jaw dropped at Ben's car.

"Nice try, Aiden. This car probably cost more than our entire house. How was school?"

"It was good—but whose car?"

Ben, who had taken several steps back and was leaning against the tall oak tree beside the driveway, trying to appear casual, stepped toward the car. "Mine. Do you want to see the inside?"

"Aiden, this is an old friend. His name is Ben. Ben, this is Aiden, my oldest; Mark, my middle child; and Autumn, my youngest—my wild child. Kids, say hi to Ben."

"Hi, Ben," the kids said almost simultaneously, obeying their mother while bouncing excitedly around and closely examining the external details of the fancy new car in their driveway.

"Hey, guys. Nice to meet you. I knew your mom in high school. Wanna see something cool?" Ben clicked a button on the key fob, and the convertible top began to fold in upon itself, opening it up to allow for closer inspection of the interior.

"Whoa! I bet this goes fast!" Aiden said, gazing in awe at the digital settings on the vehicle's dashboard.

"It does," Ben said with a grin, "but never past the speed limit. Safety first." Ben winked at Gia as he opened the driver-side door and ushered the kids inside.

"We can go in?" asked Aiden. "Really?"

"Of course. Go ahead. Maybe someday your mom will let me take you all for a ride. Maybe out for ice cream." Ben nudged Gia with his elbow as the kids cheered, indicating their approval. Aiden sidled into the driver's seat, making "vroom" sounds as he pretended to drive the car.

Ben

Ben stared at Aiden sitting in the vehicle, assessing and taking in his features. *It really is a remarkable resemblance.* There was no denying that Aiden was his son. He wondered if the boy had noticed the similarities between himself and his mother's "old friend" but assumed it wasn't something he would pick up on immediately... especially when distracted by the luxury vehicle.

As the children played in his car, Gia seemed nervous that they'd break something expensive. "Aiden, be careful with the settings. Don't touch anything," she said.

"Gia, it's okay. I don't care. It's just a car," Ben reassured her. While it *was* his pride and joy as far as material possessions went, he saw they were thoroughly enjoying themselves. A car could be repaired. The odds of the kids breaking something expensive or difficult to fix were slim, and if they did—they did. One of the benefits of being financially secure was that he didn't have to worry too much about the financial burdens of "the little things," like auto repairs.

They say money can't buy happiness—and that's true—but it can make certain aspects of life a whole lot easier, he thought. *It could make Gia's life a whole lot easier.*

After the novelty wore off and the kids began showing traces of boredom with the car, Gia announced it was time to head inside. She ushered them out of the driver's side door one by one. "I'll be inside in just a few minutes, guys. There are snacks in the fridge. You can watch TV or use your tablets until I get in shortly; then, it's homework time for anyone with it. Aiden, help the little kids if they need anything," Gia told them. "I'm just going to say goodbye to Ben for a few minutes."

"Gia, they're all perfect. Aiden is amazing. I can't possibly thank you enough for letting me meet him. I want to be in his life. Whatever happens between you and me, please let me get to know him better." Tears formed in the corners of Ben's eyes, threatening a deluge of emotions long pent up. He couldn't believe he'd let so many years pass without meeting Aiden. He had so much to catch up on, and he decided to be there for him, Gia, and the other kids through whatever may come.

They deserve that from me. It's the least I can do after everything.

For the Kids

GIA

Chapter 40

BEN REACHED out and held Gia's hand for a moment. "Thank you," he repeated.

Gia's eyes began to well up with tears, so she looked away and muttered a quick "You're welcome" before taking a step away from the car to allow Ben access. "They seem to like you—and your car," she added as Ben reached around her for a hug.

"Can I see you again soon?"

Gia lingered in the hug, pressing the side of her cheek against his chest. "I mean, we're going to be trial partners in a business, so I imagine you'll be seeing a lot of me," Gia added, a smile creeping across her features as she teased.

"You know that isn't what I meant. I want to see you again

under strictly non-business circumstances." As Ben spoke, he walked his fingers downward until his hand lingered on the lower portion of Gia's back, resting just above her behind.

"Benjamin, are you trying to torture me?" Gia rolled her eyes and referencing his wandering hand.

"That depends. Is it working?"

"Maybe," Gia said breathlessly.

"Good." Ben brushed his lips across the top of her ear before pulling away suddenly, giving Gia a quick peck on the cheek and climbing into his car. "We can finish this up another time," he said, winking.

Gia huffed, folding her arms across her chest. "That was mean. You're mean." She realized he remembered that her ears were sensitive to his kiss and that he knew exactly what he was doing with that move.

"Business lunch at *Charmed* the day after tomorrow?" Ben asked through the driver's side window.

"Mmmhmm," Gia responded, spinning on her heel and walking toward the house.

"I'll text you later," Ben yelled.

Without turning to face him, Gia gave a quick side wave, then pulled open the front door to greet the chaos of her children.

Ben

I love that woman. God, do I love that woman! Ben thought, tuning the satellite radio station to fit his mood. Having planned to be out with Gia most of the day, Ben had completed all the most critical business items and, for the first time in a while, had a bit of "free time" he wasn't about to waste.

Before pulling away, he pulled out his phone and scanned his contact list, rubbing his chin thoughtfully. "Bingo!" he said aloud, pushing to dial a number and listening to the phone ring.

"Hey, man!" a male voice answered. "You still with Gia?"

"Hey, Matt. I'm just leaving. Listen, are you and Carla still at the restaurant? I may need your help with something..."

"Yeah, we are. We may, uh, we may need your help, too," Matt said, a plea which was met by a squeal of laughter from Carla in the background. "We might need you—or someone—to drive Gia's car—and us—home."

"How come? What's wrong—oh," Ben cut himself off, realizing the two were likely drunk from one too many complimentary beverages at *Charmed to Table*. "I see how it is. Drinking me right out of business, are we?" A grin crept across Ben's face as he turned his car on with the touch of a button, switching the call to Bluetooth.

"It was a celebration," Matt said. "You said so yourself! By the way, are we celebrating anything else? How'd it go with the kids?"

"Just fine. That's part of what I need your help with. I'll explain when I get there in a few... and stop drinking! I need you both at least minimally coherent." Ben pulled the car back onto the street and headed in the direction of the downtown area toward *Charmed*. He had an idea, but he'd need guidance from the people who knew Gia's children best—her best friends.

૨♠

Carla

"He says we are supposed to wait for him," Matt began. "He wants help." Then, he burst out laughing. "And we're supposed to stop drinking."

Carla cackled, knowing she was teetering precariously close to drunk. "Maybe we did go a little too far with testing the cocktails." She grinned at Matt from across the table. "I wonder what he wants help with."

"I bet it involves Gia. Anyone can see he's still in love with the woman. Not to mention she's the mother of his child."

"The child he didn't want until now, apparently," Carla reminded Matt.

"We all make mistakes. He's trying to fix it, it seems." The two went back and forth, discussing Ben's intentions, until he appeared in the doorway, grinning at them.

"Well, hello there," Carla said, raising a glass and stumbling over her words. "We're still here!'

"I see that," said Ben, chuckling. "I don't care if you drink or don't drink right now—but you're going to help me! I have an idea." Carla and Matt gazed quizzically at Ben momentarily, expecting him to continue.

"Okay, what's the idea?" Carla finally blurted out.

"I want a brand-new kids menu before Gia comes back to take over—food and dessert—and I want to base it off Gia's children's favorite foods and themes! I know Aiden is into cars, right? We can work with that! What else? What do Mark and Autumn like?"

Carla squealed with excitement. "Gia will *love* this. Her kids are her world. And the kids will love it, too. We desperately need a restaurant with a truly family-friendly menu around here. We don't have kids, but so many of our friends do, and there are so few places to celebrate special moments where the kids *and* parents can enjoy the menu."

"Agreed," Matt said. "Mark is into superheroes. Autumn is into all that girly stuff—unicorns, pink, dolls, sparkles, I don't even know what—"

"FALL! Autumn loves Halloween, and all things fall—maybe it's because of her name, I don't know. But what about some year-round fall-themed options?"

"I love it," Ben said. "So... okay. Mark's Superhero Smores? Aiden's Corvette Key Cake Pops? Autumn leaf sugar cookies? I'm just going off the top of my head here. I need you guys to put more thought into this—I'll pay you, of course!"

Carla rolled her eyes. "I'm pretty sure you've already paid us significantly over our pay rate in cocktails and food today," she said with a chuckle. "We got this. Right, Matty?"

"Yep. Give us tonight to think about it. We'll get you some more ideas," Matt agreed.

"I want to set up the whole menu, get some samples printed, and surprise Gia with it. If she likes it, we'll move the concept forward."

"Move the concept forward." Carla snorted. "You sound so professional—like a real businessperson or something." Ben lifted his hand and gestured to the space around them, giving Carla a nod. "Oh. Right. I guess you *are* a businessman. Sorry."

Ben grinned, thinking about the many hotels and eco-resorts he'd opened globally, not to mention the restaurant and café locally. "I dabble." He chuckled. "Now, for the surprise component... I'm going to need your help..." Ben leaned in and began quietly discussing logistics and ideas with Carla and Matt. Occasional squeals of excitement erupted from the table as their menu reveal plan—among other things—was fleshed out.

"Gia is going to lose her mind over this—maybe even her heart," Carla said, breathing in deeply and letting out a long whistle as she let out the air.

Trouble in Paradise

GIA

TWO DAYS LATER, Gia parked and made her way to *Charmed to Table,* where she was to meet Ben for a business lunch, followed by a non-business date. He wouldn't tell her the latter's details but expressed that it was to remain strictly business-free. Gia couldn't help but wonder what he had in mind, especially since Carla had been scarce since Ben returned her and Matt—and Gia's car—following their free lunch at the restaurant. *Come to think of it,* she realized, *they'd all been acting weird and distant.*

As she approached the restaurant's doors, she was startled by an unexpected female voice. There, hovering near the entrance to *Charmed to Table,* was Jen, the woman Ben had been with the day he'd run into Carla, Matt, and her. "I hope you aren't going in to see Ben," the woman purred, batting her heavily lined eyes. "Oh, he didn't tell you?" A smug smile crossed her lips.

"Hello, Jen. Uh, lovely to see you again," Gia was able to muster despite the disdain she felt over seeing this woman again. "Tell me what?"

"Oh, how positively cruel of him to leave you hanging like this. You must have misinterpreted something. As it turns out, Ben and I are giving it another go. In fact, we're about to leave for our date right now to—you know," she said, winking, "rekindle our brief connection behind closed doors." Gia's jaw dropped. How could he do this? And after meeting Aiden?

"I-I-I—" Gia stuttered, unable to put her feelings into words.

"Yes, I know. It came as a surprise to me, too, when Ben called me out of the blue and asked me to meet him here," Jen continued, but her words seemed rushed. "I'll certainly tell him you stopped by to see him, but maybe it's better if you leave now."

Gia didn't know what to say or do. She was stunned. "We—uhm, we had a meeting. For work," she managed, blinking back tears that threatened to pour like a torrent down her face.

"Yes, yes. Of course. It probably slipped his mind. He can give you a call to reschedule for another time. He probably just forgot to call and cancel after we spoke. He was a little distracted, and—how do I say this? Hot and bothered," Jen whispered. "Bye, now!" Jen said, waving as a cue for Gia to leave.

Gia was shaking from head to toe and could no longer hold back the tears. She turned on her heel and walked away in the direction of her car. As soon as she reached it, she climbed in, clutched the steering wheel and started sobbing.

Ben

Where is she? Ben asked himself, glancing out the front doors as he moved to the front of the restaurant. *She should be here by now. She's always early.*

Ben glanced at his phone, checking the time, before peering out the doors again. *Yep. Late.* He pulled up her phone number, and it began to ring, but there was no answer. As he walked toward the front of the restaurant, a woman sitting alone at the bar with a familiar face and striking features caught his eye.

"Jen!" Ben exclaimed, surprised to see her there. "What—what are you doing here?"

"Oh, Benji!" she said, feigning surprise at seeing him there. "Fancy meeting you here. It must be fate," she purred.

"That, or you're still following me," Ben said, rolling his eyes. "Jen, I told you... If you keep this up, I will have to get the police involved. I'm not interested. You keep showing up, and I keep telling you I'm not interested. You're not even supposed to be in this restaurant."

Jen stood up from her seat at the bar and folded her arms across her chest. "It's because of that dirty little garden ho, Gia, isn't it? What does she have that I don't?" Hearing those words, Ben glared at Jen, holding her gaze.

"Listen, you don't say another word about Gia—ever. She's more of a woman than you'll ever be. She loved me *without* knowing I owned this restaurant. *Without* knowing that the fancy car out front belongs to me. She loved me before any of that existed, with no strings attached. I know she did. Now, when she arrives, I will continue proving to her how much I love her back—and how I'll never hurt her or her family again. Now, leave. Leave before I make you leave."

Taken aback, Jen rolled her eyes at Ben. "You'll be sorry," she muttered beneath her breath.

"What was that?" he asked.

"Oh, nothing. But I don't think you'll be seeing much of your little garden friend again. I just saw her leaving not so long ago—and she didn't look pleased."

Ben glared. "Jen, what did you do?"

"Oh, nothing. Nothing that impacts me, anyway." She smirked. "Good luck, Benji." Jen strutted toward the doors and exited the restaurant without another word, leaving Ben staring at her in shock.

"Shit," Ben said. "Shit, shit, shit!" He gazed out the window, watching Jen climb into her car and drive off, knowing she'd said something to Gia to keep her from their meeting and Ben in general. Without another thought, he ran to the back of the restaurant, grabbed his briefcase, then rushed out the door and ran to his car while dialing his phone.

"Hello? Ben? Why are you calling me? Why aren't you with Gia?" Carla asked as she picked up the call.

"I can't explain now. Jen told her something—I'm not exactly sure what—but she isn't here. I don't think she's coming. I need you and Matt to help me find her. I can't lose her again before I even *have* her." Ben sounded frantic as he explained the situation to Carla as best he could without knowing many of the details himself.

"Okay, okay, you've got it. Where should we look?"

"I'm checking the parking areas. Our meeting wasn't supposed to be too long ago, so maybe she hasn't left downtown yet. You know her better than anyone. Check the places she loves. Check the places she'd go to think. I don't know. Just—wait— never mind. Don't go anywhere. I'll call you back."

As Ben pulled into the municipal parking lot, he saw her car first, then looked more closely to see her crouched over the steering wheel, her body making the telltale lurching motions to indicate one thing—she was crying. Sobbing, actually. He parked in an available space and ran to her car, knocking on the driver's side window to get her attention.

Gia looked up, red-faced, tears streaming down her face. Upon realizing it was Ben, she turned the key in the ignition, starting the car and mouthed the word "NO" at him. He knocked again, this time more desperately, and Gia noticed the terrified look on his face. She tilted her head, taking in his expression, then rolled the window down just a crack.

"What do you want?" she asked, wiping tears away with her sleeve.

"You, Gia. I want you. God, you know I want you."

"What about Jen?" A pained look crossed Gia's face as she sniffled.

"Jen is nothing to me. She has been following me around. Somehow, she discovered that I'm worth more than she originally thought—not as a person, though, only financially. She hasn't left me alone since, but I swear there's nothing there. She's awful."

"Why didn't you tell me?"

"I didn't think it mattered. After a bit more time being ignored, I thought she'd just get bored and go away. I never thought she'd involve you. I'm so sorry. I don't know what she told you, but I'm sorry it hurt you."

Gia's eyes threatened another torrential downpour as Ben gazed into them. "Gia, let me get in. I want to take you somewhere. And I have something to show you. In a way, we're about to combine the business meeting with the date, which I swore I wouldn't do, but... this hasn't exactly gone how I'd planned today."

Gia nodded slowly and hit the unlock button on the car door, causing it to make a clicking sound she'd expected would prompt Ben to get in—but he didn't move.

"Let me drive. You're upset... And, this part was supposed to be a surprise, anyway," Ben said, gripping the door handle, pulling it open, and gesturing for Gia to move to the other side.

Blind Surprises

GIA

Chapter 42

Gia stepped from the car and walked around the front to the passenger side, opening the door and climbing in. She pulled the seatbelt across her lap and glanced over at Ben, who still looked concerned but was clearly trying to maintain a sense of composure.

"I just have to send a quick text," he said. "Things sort of have been... sped up. The timing and whatnot—but we should be fine. Our dinner plans just became our lunch plans, is all." Ben pulled out his phone and typed several lines of a message into a text, hit send, then put the car in reverse, not waiting for a response.

"Where are we going?" Gia asked, still a little shaky from the emotional afternoon.

"You'll see. It's someplace you know very, very well."

Gia glanced at Ben, too tired to hide her confusion. "We've already been to the botanical garden. I don't get out much anymore... where else could—"

"You'll see," Ben interrupted. "But, unfortunately for you, not right now." A slight smile formed on his lips as he handed Gia a blindfold. "Put it on—and don't peek. We can't have you ruining the surprise!"

"Ben, is this really necessary? It's been a long day, and it's not even 2 PM."

"Yes, it is. And you'll go along with it because I put a lot of effort into this date—even if it'll be a little different than I'd originally planned."

Gia scoffed and slid the blindfold over her head until it covered her eyes completely.

"Can you see anything?" Ben asked.

"Nope. Not a thing," Gia reported. Ben glanced over and stuck up his middle finger at Gia, knowing she'd call him out on it if she could see. Nothing. Silence.

"Perfect. You've passed the test," he said.

"Why? What'd you do?"

"Oh, nothing. Don't worry about it," Ben teased as he followed the roads out of the downtown area and toward the calmer, suburban areas. "Sit back and relax. It's not far."

"What isn't far?"

"Oh, nothing."

Gia sighed. "Okay, okay. I get it. You're not going to tell me. Can you at least put some music on? I can't see the radio." Ben nodded and fiddled with the radio dials, momentarily forgetting how to work Gia's car's less technologically advanced controls.

"This is good. I like this song," Gia said, and Ben returned his hand to the steering wheel. Normally, Gia would have questioned why Ben hadn't taken her hand and held it as he had on the way home from the botanical gardens the other day, but it had been a tough morning. Neither she nor Ben knew how to behave under the circumstances. She hadn't even decided whether she could believe his story about Jen, but at the same time, she felt he'd earned the chance to prove himself and his intentions."

After several minutes of silence, with the exception of the radio, the car drew to a stop.

"Don't move," Ben ordered. "I have to see something... you're still being watched!"

"Don't be creepy!" Gia said, chuckling slightly.

"I'm not. You're just under surveillance while I make sure everything is ready. Isn't that right?"

"That's right!" Matt's unexpected voice chimed in. "Mask stays on!"

"Matt? What are you doing here? I mean, wherever we are? Where are we?"

"I'm just the help," Matt said with a shrug. "You'll have to present your questions to the management. And he just walked away... but don't worry, it'll all be clear soon enough!"

Ben

"Carla, it's perfect. Thank you." Ben stood in Gia's backyard, surrounded by her breathtaking garden. Before them, a table was laid out, beautifully set with a sage green tablecloth, crystal glasses, and floral dishes, and in the center rested a vase of fresh-cut flowers and herbs from the garden, lending an intoxicating aroma to the dining area.

A TV screen was placed several feet from the table area and beautifully decorated with garlands made from various natural materials, allowing it to fit better with the serene surroundings.

"You're welcome! What the hell happened at the restaurant? Do you know how hard it was to pull all this together so many hours sooner than I'd planned?!"

"I know. I'm sorry. It was—well, Jen," Ben said, rolling his eyes. "I told you she wouldn't leave me alone, but she crossed the line this time by involving Gia directly. Anyway, I'll worry about that problem later. I think it's time to rescue Gia from her blindfold!"

"Oh my God, she actually let you make her wear it?" Carla cackled.

"I think she was tired from the sequence of events earlier—and the crying. So much crying. She really didn't even give me a hard time about it."

"She's either in love with you, or Jen did a number on her."

"Let's hope for the former..." Ben said. "Is the food here? And the video is ready?"

"All set. Ready to go. Get her in here, then we'll make the magic happen," Carla said, grinning at Ben, who was taking a deep breath to prepare.

"You know, I've given hundreds of presentations to some of the wealthiest, most powerful men and women on the planet—and somehow, this feels scarier."

"It's cause you love her." Carla placed a hand on Ben's shoulder. "Don't worry, Benji. Matty and I are rooting for ya!"

"Thanks. I couldn't have done this without you guys, especially with today's unexpected sequence of events. On that note, let's go get our little gardener!"

"Our dirty hoe," Carla added.

"Watch it. That's my future girlfriend you're talking about... I hope, anyway," Ben said, placing his hand against the table to steady himself as he prepared to get Gia from the car.

"You've combined her three favorite things—her children, her garden, and fresh food- into the perfect date and a gift she'll be reminded of daily! Not to mention a dream vacation, career opportunity as a partner at *Charmed* and the potential for financial security. If she says no, I'll date you!" Carla joked.

"Yeah, that'll go over great with Matt."

"Eh, he'll get over it," Carla said, dismissively waving her hand. "Okay, enough joking. Go get your girl!"

Happy Endings

GIA

Chapter 43

"ALRIGHT, MATT. YOU'RE OFF-DUTY," Ben said as he returned to Gia's car and opened the door, taking her hand in his. As she went to remove the blindfold, he stopped her. "Nope. I don't think so. Not yet. Soon." He helped her rise from her seat in the car, then held both hands to lead her, acting as her eyes.

"Ben, don't you think this is getting a little ridiculous now? I can't see a thing," Gia whined.

"As it should be. All part of the plan, my dear."

Gia could feel the pink flush into her cheeks as Ben said, "My dear." The words were simple and innocent, but she hadn't heard him say them in many years. Her reaction surprised her, triggering a weakening combination of nostalgia and desire. She used his shoulder to steady herself and get her bearings. "Oh, I—the blindfold. It's hard to balance," she said, lying.

Ben chuckled, seeing right through her. "Mmhmm," he said. "Hold my hands, follow where I lead."

As Ben led Gia to the backyard, he was surprised she didn't immediately know where they were. It was interesting just how important the role of one single sense—sight—could be. Soon, though, Gia breathed deeply through her nose, taking in the sweet aromas of her flowers and herbs dancing on the breeze. Ben could tell she had a general idea of where she was—a garden—if not the full knowledge that it was, in fact, *her* garden.

"Where are we? It's so familiar, but it feels so strange not to see. Are we—" Gia stopped speaking when her feet caught on one of the slightly raised paving stones that led to her patio. She knew that stone. She had tripped on it several times that year, always saying she'd fix it the next time she had a free moment in the garden—but somehow never got around to it.

"Why are we—" Gia began.

"You'll see," Ben whispered. "It's a surprise. Follow me." He kissed the top of her ear, just as he had the other day. Her body shook as if it had sent shivers throughout. When they arrived at the table, Ben pulled a chair for Gia and guided her to sit. As he did so, he flipped on the TV screen using a remote resting in front of his place setting. Music filled the garden area, and he slowly removed the blindfold from Gia's face, allowing her to see the extraordinarily decorated garden and dining area.

Gia's jaw dropped. "Wow—you?"

"And Carla and Matt. A few things had to get moved around. Pretend it's just before dusk. There were supposed to be twinkle lights, fake stars, and fireflies, but this will be just as good. Are you ready?"

"Ready for what?"

"Watch." Ben gestured to the TV screen. Ben hit a button on the remote, and the music became softer. The screen illuminated with images of Gia's garden amidst the background sound of children's laughter. The camera zoomed in on three children at play in the yard, then focused on one—Aiden.

"If I could have anything I wanted on a children's menu," Aiden said, "I would choose chicken nuggets—but in the shape of cars!" Aiden's smile grew large as he held up a chicken nugget in the shape of a race car, then another in the other hand unmistakably shaped like a VW Beetle.

Gia laughed. "Oh my gosh! I love that." Ben paused the video as a waiter emerged from the sliding glass door and walked to the table carrying a platter full of car-shaped chicken nuggets.

"Dinner is served," Ben announced. "But, save room. It's going to be a bit of a long meal. We are developing a long history of making attempts to try everything on the menu—why stop now?"

"What menu is this?" asked Gia.

"I give you the brand-new *Gia's Charmed to Table* Children's Menu. I think you'll find it hits very close to home. Eat your nuggets while you watch." Ben hit the play button again.

Mark's face filled the screen next. He held what looked to be a smore in his hands, but one large marshmallow had been cut into three sections—one red, one white, and one blue. Two graham crackers were on each side like a regular campfire smore, but a piece of white chocolate was beneath each. It had an unmistakable superhero vibe to it.

"Superhero Smores!" Mark shouted, flinging his Superman cape over his shoulder and raising the smore skyward. "The dessert of superheroes!"

His toothy smile made Gia laugh. He'd always been such a sugar junky, it wasn't surprising he picked a dessert. Again, Ben paused the video, and a waiter arrived with all the materials needed to make the smores right at the table, including a mini campfire and stakes to toast the marshmallows!

"Ben, this is amazing!" Gia squealed.

"Lightly toasted, burnt, or flaming?" the waiter asked, grinning.

"Ball of fire," Gia said. "But I don't think that should be one of the options at the restaurant."

"No, no," Ben began. "This is just for us. No rules here!"

As the chef prepared a plateful of smores, Ben clicked the video on again.

"I'm Autumn. If I could make a kids' menu, I'd make sure it had pancakes. But, special pancakes for each season or holiday. Snowflake and snowman pancakes in winter, maybe Christmas, Leaves and pumpkins in the fall, suns in the summer, you know —like that! Maybe flavors, too."

Autumn reached down and lifted a platter of pancakes toward the camera. Many were shaped like different seasonal shapes, while others were decorated with cookie frosting and sweets to make them fit their themes. As Autumn lifted the plate, she couldn't help but grab the Christmas tree-shaped pancake and dip it into a "snowbank" of whipped cream, stuffing it into her mouth.

Gia laughed at her wild child's antics. "Ben, this is perfect," Gia announced as a platter of pancakes arrived. Ben stopped pausing the video and letting it play out, knowing that each food and drink option would eventually be brought to the table for sampling. It was a complete menu of appetizers, entrees, and desserts curated by kids!

When the video ended and the table was laden with food, Gia shook her head in shock.

"How'd you manage to interview the kids?" Gia asked curiously.

"Carla, again," Ben said. "You thought she had been ignoring your calls, probably. But the past couple of days have been hectic for her. She had to strategically get you out of the house WHILE situating herself to watch them for long enough to finish the videos. Matt helped, too. It's a good thing he knows his way around a camera. Quite frankly, my dear, it was a logistical night-mare—but well worth it."

Gia grinned and began to eat more of the food that surrounded her.

"It's all locally sourced, so it fits the *Charmed to Table* model. You're, of course, welcome to adjust, remove, or add anything you want. We pulled this together very, very quickly."

"Ben, it's perfect. I love it. I don't want to change a thing!"

"Well, good. We won't have to do too much work on these menus," said Ben as he pulled a design proof of the new menu out from beneath the table. The menu featured hand-drawn superheroes, race cars, seasonal items, and more.

"Is this—?"

"Yeah, your kids did the art, too. They're really excited—and when they get home in an hour, I'm sure they'll be more than ready to eat some of the rest of this food under Carla and Matt's watchful eyes while you and I go somewhere quiet to talk. I have one more surprise..."

"Ben! No more surprises. This is unbelievable. This is perfect. How did you do all this? Why did you do all this for me?"

"Gia, you know the answer to that question. You've always known it. I love you. I've never stopped loving you through everything. Leaving you behind wound up being the biggest regret of my entire life. Now, I want us to have the start we should have had in the first place." Ben stood up from his chair, walked over to Gia's side of the table, and leaned downward. He got down on a knee.

"Ben, no. No, don't."

"Don't what?" Ben asked. "Oh. OH! No, no. No. I'm not asking you to marry me! I just—I—wow—pretend that didn't just happen. I was just trying to—" Ben finally managed to stop talking and show Gia his intention by lifting the wide vase of cut flowers. There, beneath the vase, were seven plane tickets.

"Gia, will you go to Brazil with me? For a vacation. All of you —even Carla and Matt. To the original eco-lodge. I want to share it with you. I... I still own that first one. I couldn't let it go."

"Oh my gosh, Ben!" Gia struggled to hold back tears. She'd

spent her entire adult life feeling like she'd missed the travel opportunity of a lifetime. All the pieces of her life she thought she'd missed out on were falling into place—all because of Ben.

"Yes," Gia finally said. "Yes, I'd love to go to Brazil with you, my love. I love you."

"I love you, too, my dirty hoe. Does this mean we can delete our *Only Gardeners* accounts now?"

"YES!"

About the Author

Regina Bergen is an avid gardener—and can't even count the number of times she's said, "It's not an autobiography!" in reference to *Dirty Hoe – A Gardening Romance*, the first book in the Small Town Dirt series.

Regina lives with her three children and two rescue dogs in the beautiful Hudson Valley region of New York. She has a B.A. in Environmental Studies and Latin American Studies and a Master's in Public Administration.

Before she began writing and editing full-time, Regina worked as a fundraiser at a global environmental conservation organization and spent several years as a stay-at-home mom. She loves the outdoors, animals, cooking, coffee, and spending her free time with her kids and pets.

Social Media:
    Facebook: Regina Bergen Author
    Email: WritingByRegina@gmail.com